SANDPEOPLE

SANDPEOPLE

Hal Barwood

*what happens following the events
chronicled in **Glitterbush***

an astromechanical adventure

Sandpeople

Copyright © 2020 Hal Barwood
All rights reserved
A Finite Arts Book
Published by Finite Arts LLC, Portland, Oregon
version 2.1

ISBN 978-1-7354222-0-6

This is a work of fiction. The State of Arizona, the Palo Verde Nuclear Generating Station, KTVK, Great Zimbabwe National Park, Mexico's National Museum of Anthropology, the ancient city of Teotihuacan, and the statue of Coatlicue are all real; but the locations, communities, and enterprises depicted herein are either fictional in themselves or fictional in detail. All the characters and incidents in this fictional world are products of the author's imagination. No resemblance to any real institution, person, or alien is intended.

Acknowledgments . . .

Many thanks to the readers willing to read unfinished versions of this tale: Barbara, Jonathan, and Tobias Barwood; Betsy and Curt Blanchard; Robert Dalva; Noah Falstein; Beverly Graves; Tony Hsieh; Lee Sheldon

Thanks always to Google, Wikipedia, and the rest of the World Wide Web for cataloging the internet's facts — actual, alternative, fake, and fantastical . . .

About the Author . . .

Hal Barwood is a veteran writer with multiple credits in multiple media. Find out more here . . .

www.finitearts.com

with love for

Oliver

stay curious, kiddo

Table of Contents

Phase 1

1

SPACE, ladies and gentlemen — all you want between the stars, barely enough in this room. Life — rare out there, awfully crowded here. Find a seat if you can, please, we've got a lot to talk about."

A junior army officer was pacing the dais of a spartan briefing room in the Pentagon, attempting to call an important meeting to order. After the crowd of Washington officials, milling and gossiping, shuffled into the available chairs, Army Major General Russell Congreve stood up to take the floor. He was tall and thin and fit at fifty-five years of age, an Afghanistan combat veteran, with silver hair on his head, two silver stars on his shoulders, and a narrow mustache on his lip.

"Ladies and gentlemen, fellow officers, distinguished members of Congress and the Administration, I have some information to divulge that will be real news to many of you. So, before I continue, please understand that what we will be discussing today is a *Special Access Program,* and is classified *Top Secret* as such."

The general pointed, and the junior officer with him dimmed the lights. A wide screen behind the dais lit up with a map of southern Arizona. Virtual push pins appeared here and there around the city of Tucson.

"What you see here are the locations where our first visitors from another world were discovered."

Some members of the audience already knew the headlines. Gasps issued from those who did not.

Congreve managed a thin smile. "Yes, that's right — living things not of this Earth. Initial discovery by a local rancher some twelve years ago."

One of the pins blinked to call attention to an area west of the city.

"Quite a few more have been found since then, most of them near Tucson, but a few as far away as Turkey and Spain."

Murmurs of astonishment welled up from the assembly.

Congreve paused to study his audience, gauging preconceptions. He scratched his mustache.

"Now these things, these entities, they are not what you think. When we imagine space aliens — we think of monsters, right? Little green men, the greys, big eyes, or lovable ET. But instead, what arrived on our doorstep were . . . I know how this sounds . . . *plants.*"

More murmurs and doubtful grumbles were heard.

"Not your everyday vegetables, however. These plants are made out of metallic crystals. The leaves, if you call them that, are highly efficient solar cells."

Dubious snorts and coughs greeted this pronouncement.

Congreve grinned sardonically. "I know the feeling. Hard to swallow. Imagine my thoughts when I was first told this improbable tale."

He pointed again to the junior officer, who left the dais and returned wearing rubber gloves. He was cradling a ceramic pot that held a glittering plant about a foot in diameter.

"This — this shiny little bush — this is what we're talking about."

Someone in the back of the room lost all patience. "That's a model you've got there, right?"

"No sir. This is the real thing. It's been growing, although very slowly, in our lab for a couple of years now."

"Someone else raised a hand and blurted, "DNA analysis? Have you published anything?"

Congreve shook his head. "These things do not contain a shred of DNA. Like us, they're composed of billions of cells, but the cells are tiny crystals, and they look like . . . well, beach sand."

"Are they dangerous? Are you risking our lives here?"

"The answer is yes and no. As long as you don't get tangled up in a big one, they are inert. Each one gradually produces a potato-size component, and when components merge we have seen some autonomous activity."

"They grow creatures?"

"Mechanical entities. Robots if you will."

"Holy Mother of God."

Congreve paused to consider any further disclosures. At length he decided to push on. "To be perfectly candid, the bushes have — how shall I put it? — parasitic qualities. So, yes, there is an obvious element of danger. Contact has been known, in a few isolated cases, to transform humans into something else . . . aliens, if you will."

Howls of protest.

"Before you panic, be aware — one such transform gave us the means to combat and defeat these things, should they eventually prove hostile."

The junior officer removed a long metal tube and a power pack from a case on the floor of the dais. He handed the tube to Congreve and pressed a button. Little green LEDs lit up on the power pack. Congreve hefted the tube as if it were a combat rifle, activated a laser sight, steadied the beam on the alien entity, and pulled a trigger. The bush began vibrating wildly and suddenly dissolved into a pile of sand.

Roars of amazement.

Congreve made a little bow. "There you have it. Microwaves disrupt communication between the crystalline cells. Earth is saved. Life as we know it goes on."

A cacophony of questions and demands arose in the audience as the junior officer used a vacuum cleaner to collect the sandy residue.

Congreve raised both his hands to quiet the gathering. "Now I'd like to fill you in on the background, on the latest developments — what we know, what we've been doing about this unusual situation. So, to start, please welcome Dr. Nancy Weatherall. She's an astronomer at the University of California in Berkeley."

A dumpy woman in a shapeless tweed jacket rose from the audience and strode to the lectern. She was getting on in years and, if not for the excitement of recent developments, was ready for retirement. She donned a pair of owlish glasses to consult her notes, signaled with a finger, and the image on the screen behind her darkened. Now everyone was staring at little points of light, a star field.

"The night sky, folks. For those of you who don't get out too often, you're looking at the constellation Taurus, in the zodiac, a segment of the ecliptic plane."

Weatherall signaled again, and a white circle appeared around one of the less impressive points.

"The star I've circled has no name, and goes by the designation PCNSO-621371-K in the Public Catalog of Nearby Stellar Objects. As per that designation, it's an old K-type star, smaller than our Sun and a lot dimmer. It's sitting just about eleven light years away, local by astronomical standards, yet impossibly distant for the kind of rockets that got us to the Moon. We believe one of the planets orbiting this star is the origin of our bushes, sent on their way a hundred years ago."

An enlarged image of the star faded into view, revealing its orange color.

"As you might imagine, we have become very curious about this extraterrestrial solar system. In the years since we first began tracking down funny plants, we have also commandeered a number of major telescopes. Perhaps some of you recall the temporary maintenance problems and downtimes that have been reported.

Well, there were no actual problems, no downtime. Here's what the Hubble and the VLT down in Chile were really doing . . ."

Three blurry dots swam into view near the star.

"This image represents a heroic effort — it's the very first time we've been able to photograph extra-solar planets and take their measure. All of these worlds are roughly Earth-size. The outer planet is very cold, much too far from its small parent to support life. The other two are possibilities, but the innermost planet's rotation is tidally locked. Living there would be a challenge. The middle planet is hotter and dryer than Earth, but theoretically orbiting within the habitable zone. We're puzzled, because we find little air, no oxygen, and only the faintest trace of water vapor, all necessary for the kind of biology we know and represent."

Weatherall lifted a finger to bring her slide show to an end.

"In summary, I think we can say that whoever decided to sow their seeds on Planet Earth are not very much like us."

She stepped down from the dais, waving to acknowledge a ragged spasm of applause.

General Congreve resumed his position at the lectern. A map of the world appeared on the TV screen. One by one, another series of virtual push pins dropped onto the map, showing where bushes had been discovered. Over the course of a minute, clusters formed. Soon the map was covered with dots. A number in large type faded in: **135**.

Congreve pointed at the accumulating dot total. "For the past three years I've been running *Operation Wild Harvest,* locating and collecting these bushes. In the first year we found seventy-nine. In the second, fifty-six more. But last year, none at all. We launched a special reconnaissance satellite — MECOR-1 — disguised as a climate change tracker, with infrared sensors to help us search. We've spent months scouring the Earth to be sure, but we see no more blips, and it looks like we got them all.

"As a result, the Joint Chiefs, members of the Senate Select Committee on Intelligence, the National Security Council, and other stakeholders have reached a conclusion: we're standing down. Wild Harvest goes into the history books as a big success, and we can redirect some defense dollars to better purpose."

A voice from the audience interrupted: "How can you be sure?"

Congreve winced. "Well, we can't be absolutely sure, of course. And we're not giving up altogether, not letting our guard down. We're reconstituting the *Joint Powers Immigration Task Force* to continue surveillance at a more economical level. Retired General Maurice Upshaw is returning from his post at NASA Ames Research Center to lead the mission. Dr. Weatherall and other former members of the team will join him."

A woman from the State Department stood up and raised her hand. Congreve gestured to invite a comment.

"You talk about plants, General. What if these plants aren't the whole story. What if they are . . . well, you know . . . scouts?"

Congreve spread his arms out wide. "Good question."

2

DAVIS-MONTHAN Air Force Base sits on 10,500 acres of urban land within the city limits of Tucson, Arizona. There, a single long runway serves more than one hundred and fifty aircraft of several Air Force commands, including the 355th Fighter Group and its squadrons of A-10 Warthogs. The runway itself is surrounded by offices, workshops, housing, stores, schools, medical facilities, and the famous aircraft boneyard, where obsolete war planes go to die. 11,000 Air Force personnel share the base and its labors with another 11,000 civilian employees.

Late on a cool evening in early spring, three scruffy men approached the base entrance at the intersection of Craycroft and Golf Links roads. They bypassed the visitor control center in a little Nissan pickup truck, overpowered the civilian guards at the main gate, and made their way to Building 220, where they broke locks, disabled alarms, and entered a classified storage area. What they found there was a collection of small vitreous bushes growing slowly under orange-tinted lights and shelves holding plastic bags of sand.

After examining the tags identifying bag contents, they selected six of them and departed.

Base security was flummoxed. Two gate guards were dead. Autopsies were required to determine that they died from very small caliber bullet wounds. Their internal organs were shredded, suggesting explosive force.

Surveillance cameras recorded the Nissan pickup truck arriving and departing, but the license plates were obscured by the kind of translucent plastic covers designed to fool highway toll booths.

Security procedures were immediately reviewed and expanded. Entrance to the base became subject to stringent protocols involving special identification documents. Over the course of the following month, access was denied to multiple drug dealers, felons, undocumented immigrants, and sexual predators. The identity of those who made the successful intrusion, however, was not determined, and no one was arrested for perpetrating the break-in.

The security team pondered the unusual burglary — small bags of sand taken; nothing else — and wondered how such petty thievery could possibly be worth a couple of murders.

3

HARRIET CHOW, a pert Asian woman of 31 years, was a trained engineer. Gerrit Darlington Holzgraf III, 32, the scion of a very wealthy family, was a hopeful biologist. They fell in love when they both were members of Maurice Upshaw's Immigration Task Force. He liked her dark wintery eyes, her quick mind, and her wild black hair. She liked his lanky good looks, his sense of purpose, and his easy manner.

"Anniversary coming up. What do you say? Put a ring on it?"

"Ohmigod, is that rock a diamond? Okay — I mean, *YES!*"

They were unaware that General Congreve had authorized a renewal of the Task Force's franchise.

Instead, operating through their small research company in Tucson, *Darlington Energetix,* they were busy developing advanced solar cells made from the mineral perovskite. Their breakthrough was a promising form of artificial photosynthesis that generated liquid fuel stock from sunlight.

Samuel Chow, Holly's father, had found an alien bush on the family pecan ranch many years previously, one of the very first to be discovered. Holzgraf and his daughter took note of its perovskite leaves and began a research program to harness the mineral's potential. In the course of their work they discovered another bush. Placed in proximity to its own kind, the new discovery gave birth to a peculiar blob that seemed to exhibit intelligent behavior.

They presented their results to members of the ITF in the field by helping their blob to combine with a vicious alien robot. Once the two entities merged, the robot became docile, responsive, and the amateur bush hunters were invited to join the team.

Now, three years later, Chow was driving through the back streets of Tucson on a hot spring day, heading for an electrical supply company. She had a long list of items on her smartphone that were needed for the next step in artificial greenery.

She was motoring past the Home Depot, with her head lost in the clouds of power density equations, when she spotted a familiar-looking man in the megastore's parking lot. The sight sparked a jolt of adrenaline.

She continued on for a few blocks in a daze, then pulled to the curb and punched a contact on her smartphone.

"Guy? Hey, listen — I'm out here on my way, and . . . and . . . I just saw a ghost."

Holzgraf, busy in the Darlington workshop, sensed the tension in his fiancée's voice. "What's wrong, Holly? What's up?"

"Remember Jim Lockwood?"

"Sure. The alien masquerading as our teammate, who killed himself rather than betray his human friends."

"Yeah, him. Dead, right? Suicide. A pile of sand."

"Right. You sound terrible. What's bothering you?"

"Well, I just drove past the Home Depot, and who do you think I saw strolling through the parking lot?"

"I'll bite. Who?"

"Captain James Lockwood."

"Come on, hon. Can't be. You know that."

"Of course. But I saw what I saw. No joke. And unless the man had a twin brother . . ."

Holzgraf felt the hairs on the back of his neck starting to rise. He wasn't sure if he was worried that his wife-to-be was slipping a few gears, or whether she actually saw something. Those damn bushes — they were weird enough to allow anyone's imagination to run wild.

"Okay, Babe, slow down. I'm not saying you're crazy. Sure hope not. So, turn around, drive through the parking lot. Take a good look. Be careful. Don't engage. And then get back on the road and nail those power transistors we ordered."

"Yeah, will do. Stay tuned."

▼

In the few short years since its founding, Darlington Energetix had grown some, forcing a move from its shabby location on the wrong end of Grant Road to a suite in an upscale industrial building near Tucson International Airport. It now employed five people fabricating solar panels, but on this day, on a weekend, the only occupants were Chow and Holzgraf. She was trying to work, but could not sit still.

"Shit. Damn. Wrong wire."

She threw down her soldering iron, shoved the circuit board she was assembling to the side, ripped off her goggles, and embarked on an agitated tour of the Darlington premises, waving her arms and muttering.

"You know, I'm pretty sure about this. What I saw. I went back like we talked, checked the store, spotted him in the plumbing department, called his name. But then, when I got to the end of the aisle, he was gone. It really hit me. The curly dark hair, the muscles under his T-shirt . . ."

Holzgraf looked up from his computer. "Good looking guy, as I remember."

"Yeah."

"You liked him."

"Yeah, I did. But I like you a lot better."

Holzgraf frowned. "Mmm. Does this — quote, *sighting,* unquote — indicate some inner conflict, you know, about us . . ?"

Chow's dark eyes blazed. "You doubt me?"

Holzgraf registered the reproach. He opened his arms. "Come here."

They hugged. After a while the hug became a kiss. Then another. After a while they drifted toward the little bedroom built into a corner of the workshop where they kept house, loft-style.

▼

When they woke up, the bed sheets were twisted into knots, and their clothes were scattered all over the cheap Ikea rug on the floor. Chow slipped into a robe and toddled off to the adjoining bathroom.

"What do we want to do about this? Seeing Jim?" she asked.

Holzgraf looked up at the skylights overhead. The sky behind them was still bright. He checked his watch. He sighed.

"Better start at Home Depot. Maybe the guy you thought was Lockwood is an employee. Otherwise, we have no clue."

"Long shot, I know," she replied. "But I need a sanity check."

▼

They drove back across town and treated themselves to a desultory tour of Home Depot, inspecting every area, ogling every employee. Nobody looked even faintly like their former colleague.

"We need any lightbulbs today? Space heaters? Power washers?" grumbled Holzgraf.

Chow gave him a dirty look. "So he's gone. Doesn't mean he doesn't exist. Uhh . . . somewhere."

Holzgraf nodded. "No, you can't prove a negative."

They returned to Holzgraf's Jeep Wrangler and stared at the store entrance until boredom overcame them.

"What now?" asked Holzgraf, suppressing his irritation.

Chow leaned back and stared at the roof of the jeep. "We have to call Upshaw."

"Go ahead, call him."

"Except I don't have his number on my phone."

"Me neither."

Back at Darlington Energetix, Holzgraf dug Upshaw's Ames Research telephone number out of his computer database. He showed the screen to Chow.

"Okay, Babe. You saw Lockwood, you're up."

"You should call, you're better at this stuff than I am."

"Oh definitely. You know he's going to want to hear about the ray gun."

"Yeah, I'm dodging him, I admit."

"Crap."

Holzgraf slid his office chair around his beat-up desk to the company's land line, where he noted a red message light blinking. He touched a button and General Upshaw's voice blared from the loudspeaker:

"Chow? Holzgraf? I hear wedding bells. When's the big day? If you want a honeymoon, you might want to postpone. Call immediately you receive this message, day or night. Use your secure phone."

Chow and Holzgraf both scowled.

"Uh-oh. Postpone? Secure call?"

"Yeah, what's up with the grumpy old astronaut?"

Holzgraf dug into a packing box full of seldom-used gadgetry, hunting for the phone in question. Chow found a roll-around suitcase in a dark corner. She opened it, rummaged through a tangle of cables and obsolete internet modems, and tugged a bulky telephone handset free.

"Hey, got it."

She pressed a switch, but nothing happened. Holzgraf found the charger in the box he was exploring. It took half an hour before the phone's battery stored enough juice to power a call. Holzgraf dialed Upshaw's secure line, and got a cryptic response:

"This is Ames four-five-six. Leave a message, please."

"Mo? It's us. We've got some news, and I guess you do too."

Another half hour went by. Chow retreated into the office kitchen to prepare supper. Soup was bubbling on their little stove when the secure phone finally rang with Upshaw's return call. The evening meal went uneaten.

"All right you two, listen up — the big military operation, Wild Harvest? It's in the books. We're reconstituting the I-T-F as a backstop. Possibly a formality, but maybe not. So, first question: how's the weapon coming?"

Holzgraf signaled to his fiancée. "Mo wants to know about our waver," he whispered.

Chow was standing away from the phone. She cupped her hands around her mouth to make herself heard. "It's still just a prototype we slapped together. We sent it to Washington."

"Yes," noted Upshaw. "And General Congreve used it to dissolve a bush in front of a pretty good crowd of bigwigs. I was there. Very dramatic. But it's bulky, and we may need quite a few of these things."

"You sound worried, Mo. Want to tell us why?"

Chow leaned close to Holzgraf, who toggled the speakerphone button so they both could hear the general's reply.

"Well, to start — you two are formally recalled to service. You're working for me again."

"We are?"

"There was a break-in. Last week people forced their way into our storage facility at Davis-Monthan and stole some bags of the sand we're keeping there. Who would do that? Can't be an accident."

Holzgraf and Chow stared at each other.

"It was on the news," affirmed Holzgraf. "Guards were killed. But no one mentioned ITF stuff."

"No, it's classified."

The color drained from Chow's face. She grabbed the phone. "Here's something that dovetails with that — earlier today I thought I saw Jim Lockwood in the Home Depot parking lot. That's why we were calling you."

Upshaw was silent for a long moment.

"Mo? You there?"

"We've got work to do. I'll see you in Tucson in forty-eight hours."

4

GENERAL MAURICE UPSHAW, a large black man grey-
ing at the temples, was a former astronaut, one of the space shuttle
commanders. Before that he flew A-10s for the U.S. Air Force.
Like many other pilots, he retained a deep affection for the ugly
Warthogs, and today, staring out the second-story window of
Building 220, hard beside the Davis-Monthan Air Force Base runway, he was privileged to see them in action again. Four of the
attack aircraft took off as he watched, one after another in quick
succession. In less than a minute they formed into a tightly spaced
echelon formation and circled back over the base with their engines thundering. Upshaw grinned in appreciation. Then his brow
clouded over as grim memories of Iraq invaded his thoughts. His
darkening mood was mercifully interrupted by the office door
opening and voices calling his name.

He turned around, and there were Holly Chow and Guy
Holzgraf.

"Hey, Mo."

Upshaw gestured toward the runway. "They tried to kill the A-
10. The Pentagon brass counts the money, but troops on the
ground count the sorties. And now . . . what do you know? Boeing
is manufacturing new wings. Stiffer, tougher. Those pigs have got
a new lease on life."

"Like us, huh? Same mission, new tools."

Holzgraf hefted a plastic case.

"Here's the latest."

Holly popped the case open and handed Upshaw what looked
like a cross between a large handgun, a portable drill, and a small
trombone.

"You can hold this thing in one hand. The power supply — we
cobbled it together with vacuum cleaner batteries, but we've got

an order in, and the production units will have high capacity cells from Tesla, their latest battery tech."

Upshaw took the weapon and pointed it at the wall.

"No backpack. How many shots?"

"Ten, maybe twenty, before you need to swap or recharge."

"Still pretty crude. The grip is what? Pine wood?"

"Prototype Two. Our production run will have polymer components. We're rigging up a 3D printer."

"Really. Will that work?"

"We're still experimenting with the resin. If we can't compete, we'll sub the furniture from Glock."

While the trio discussed the pros and cons of the latest microwave projector, the office door opened again and a swarthy man in a rumpled suit, Dr. Roman Garibaldi, Ph.D., joined the group.

"Whatcha got there, people?" he asked.

"Oh, hi, Roman. Possible way to deploy some tactical firepower," replied Upshaw.

"That thing? Last time I zapped something we needed a trailer for the power supply. This one looks kind of puny, don't you think? Doesn't look like it could hurt the proverbial fly, let alone a raging alien monster."

Garibaldi was a professorial computer scientist in mid-career. His day job involved serving high-tech advice to federal labs from his position at *The Institute for Research on Integrated Systems,* a secretive government operation often referred to as *The IRIS Corporation.* That is, until he found a very strange bush for sale in an airport shop and raised the alarm with General Upshaw. His discovery led the general to establish the ITF.

"Dr. Skeptical," sniffed Chow.

"No," countered Garibaldi, tugging at a lock of his tousled hair, "just scared of this stuff. I want our weapons to work."

"Come on, Roman, we're using your specs, the parameters you

gave us," grumbled Holzgraf.

Garibaldi touched the weapon's metal barrel. "I like proof. Let's shoot something."

Upshaw bent over his desk and pressed a button on the intercom. "Charlie? Bring us a bush. Make it a small one."

Moments later a young Air Force sergeant appeared cradling an opaline bush between gloved hands. Following right behind him was the final member of the ITF team, Dr. Weatherall.

"Nancy," said Upshaw. "Glad you made it."

"What are you doing?" she queried. Her tone was sour.

"Ray gun demo," said Holzgraf. "Roman has doubts about us."

"Then I'm just in time. And I almost didn't make it — my dean is a very unhappy man today."

"I'll call him," said Upshaw, in an effort to smooth the social fabric. "But ITF is back in business, and we need you."

"So zap that thing for me already."

The young airman placed the little bush on the office coffee table and stepped away.

Upshaw handed the prototype weapon to Garibaldi.

"You're the doubter, doc. Fire away."

Garibaldi lifted the thing. He looked lost. "I don't know how to turn it on."

Chow reached out and flicked a switch on the barrel.

Garibaldi cautiously removed a pair of glasses from his jacket pocket and put them on. "Okay, I'm aiming. I press the trigger and — whoa, laser sight activates — press a lot harder and . . ."

Krazzz

The target bush collapsed into a pile of sparkling sand.

"Oh-ho!" exclaimed the scientist.

Weatherall came forward to examine the pile. She used a pad of paper on the table to push the grains around.

"Looks dead to me. Do these things ever regrow?"

The other team members glanced at each other.

"What do you mean?"

Weatherall snorted. "What I hear is, Holly saw our departed friend Jim Lockwood strolling around Home Depot. Last time I noticed, he resembled the pile of sand on this table."

Holly nodded. "I did see him. No kidding."

Weatherall removed her tweed jacket and threw it over a chair.

"Here's something else. My guys out at Goldstone manning NASA's deep space antennas have recorded signals coming from our favorite K-type star. First reception was logged ten months ago. They just noticed, and I just found out."

"What are they?"

"Who knows? We'd probably be sending ones and zeros, but it looks like the code uses four discrete states. The signals repeat every week or so. Without explaining anything, I asked the Cal computer science department to decrypt them." She shook her head. "*Nada.*"

"That's very odd," said Chow. "Spooky too."

"Want to hear what they sound like?"

Weatherall lifted her smartphone and tapped the audio play button. An eerie succession of flutelike tones floated through the room, blurred by a raspy layer of white noise.

"Sending signals? That's awfully expensive," mused Garibaldi. "Someone up there thinks someone down here is taking notes. Probably not us."

5

WHEN UPSHAW arrived in his office in the morning, the rest of his reconstituted team were already there noshing on breakfast snacks and fortifying themselves with bad coffee.

"Sleep well?"

Reluctant nods. None of them had fully absorbed their renewed call to service. They all missed daily lives they suspected were on indefinite, possibly permanent, hold.

Upshaw made note of the grouchy mood, motioned to the door, and a young man in uniform entered the room with a briefcase in hand.

"Say hello to Major Ochoa. And cheer up, he has some information for us."

The officer opened a briefcase and withdrew a laptop computer.

"Morning, folks. I'm the deputy director of DM security. Take a look at this video . . ."

He pressed a key on his laptop, and the ITF team clustered around the officer to see what he was talking about. The video presentation cycled through views from several surveillance cameras, all showing a late model Nissan Frontier pickup truck coming and going through the main base entrance on Craycroft Road.

"Note that the plate is unreadable. I guess you already heard about that. Now, here's another car . . ."

Video footage showed a beat-up Dodge Dart rolling past the base entrance on Golf Links Road, first in one direction, then the other. On its third pass it stopped and picked up a passenger loitering on the curb. Then it sped away north on Craycroft, following the little Nissan pickup.

Ochoa stopped the video on an image of the retreating vehicle. He pressed a key to zoom in on the license plate.

"Kind of blurry, but we have some tools . . ."

He pressed another key, and a sharpened detail of the plate appeared, revealing letters and numbers.

"Here we have a suspicious vehicle, and we made an ID. That old car is registered to one Florencio Rojas. His address is in Marana, not too far north of here."

Garibaldi pointed at the fuzzy image. "Solve your murder case?"

"Not quite. Rojas has been reported missing by his wife. She's pretty upset."

Upshaw moved to summarize the session. "Thanks for the briefing, Major. We'll put some of our own resources to work on this. Let's trade info, assuming either of us makes any further progress."

"Yes, sir."

Ochoa closed his laptop, gave the group a nod, and left the room. Upshaw dropped into his office chair. He drummed his fingers on his desktop.

"What do we think?" wondered Garibaldi. "Why would this guy — Rojas? — help steal our sandy artifacts?"

Upshaw held up a hand to forestall the question, picked up his secure phone and punched a number. "Let's see what American TV & Appliance can tell us."

A robot answered the phone. Upshaw declared his credentials, and the call was routed to a live intelligence analyst.

"Good morning, sir. How can I help you?"

"Need some information on an actor named Florencio Rojas, of Marana, Arizona. Reported missing by his wife."

"Rojas, Marana, Arizona, got it."

"Where does he work? Who does he work with? What, if anything, strikes you as odd? Any information you can provide will advance our cause."

"On it, sir. Call you back."

Weatherall spun a finger in the air to indicate perplexity. "What the heck was that?"

Upshaw shrugged. "Ammo-TV-and-App — it's a cover name for military intelligence liaison, our big-box store for secret shit."

"Are they any good?"

Upshaw smiled. "Human beings are involved. Nobody's perfect."

▼

Twenty-four hours went by.

In the interval, Holzgraf and Chow succeeded in coaxing their 3D printer to produce a polymer frame for what everyone was calling their wave gun. They were showing it off when the call from American TV & Appliance came in.

"General Upshaw — I have some news."

"Let's hear it, Lieutenant."

Upshaw pressed a button to activate his telephone speaker. The team gathered around his desk.

"Mr. Rojas works, or did work, at Aztec Rubber Recovery. It's a tire recycling outfit located in the desert off Silverbell Road, about thirty-five miles from Tucson. No reason for his disappearance came up, but he's not the only one. We have three other missing persons who worked there, pretty much the whole crew."

"Recycling takes another punch," muttered Upshaw.

"Well, no, sir, not really. The company is still in business. Satellite shows employee activity on the site."

▼

General Congreve took Upshaw's telephone call in his Pentagon office.

"Russ? Got an update for you — looks like ITF has bona fide activity in the Tucson area. Theft from our archive storage unit, and something going down at a local tire recycling operation."

"Sure about this?"

"The stolen items were the bagged remains of a former ITF member who was transformed. Another member swears she just saw the same guy walking around Home Depot."

"Resurrected? Oh, for God's sake. You, your team — get a grip."

"She's not crazy, Russ."

6

A LITTLE ROBINSON R-22 helicopter, done up in red paint, lifted off from a pad adjacent to Tucson's commercial airport with Guy Holzgraf at the controls. Sitting beside him was General Upshaw. They were airborne in an innocent civilian chopper to put eyeballs on the Aztec Rubber Recovery operation without raising too much curious attention.

"How many hours you got flogging this weed eater?" growled Upshaw into his mike. They were both wearing headsets against the engine noise roaring through the paper-thin walls of the cabin.

Holzgraf turned toward his boss, noting some discomfort.

"Hundred, hundred and ten, give or take. Don't worry, Mo, you're safe with me."

"Unh-huh. Last time you parked this bird on a mountain top with an empty gas tank."

"Three years ago. Don't rub it in." Holzgraf snapped a finger against the fuel gauge. "Tanks are full. We're good for a couple of hours."

"Right, right. Sorry, getting old, getting grumpy."

"Roger that. Got your camera? Got the radio? Spectrum analyzer?"

"Ready."

"How do you want to approach? We're about ten out from Marana."

"Let's go right up the interstate, then vector west along Paloma Valley Road. Wouldn't hurt to make it look like this is an instructional flight out of the Paloma Valley airport."

"Want me to land?"

"No, just lose some altitude and climb out again. Keep our target on my side."

Out in the desert beyond the most remote housing developments, a lonely metal building stood out against the mesquite, enclosed by an aging chain link fence. A small mountain of worn-
out tires was evident beside the dirt parking lot. A thin wisp of
smoke curled up from the pile, indicating a smoldering fire. A
square hole in the tin roof made room for a large grid-like panel
centered within coppery leaflike shapes.

"Did you see that?" said Holzgraf as they cruised by.

"Oh yes. Hold course for a couple of minutes, and let's do another pass on the far side."

On the way back they noticed a line of small shapes dotted
along the building's wall, glistening in reflected sunlight. They
were too far away to tell if they were looking at alien bushes.

In the ITF office at Davis-Monthan, Holly Chow downloaded
the surveillance data onto Nancy Weatherall's laptop.

The team gathered around for a close look.

"Well now, I'd say the Wild Harvest boys didn't find all the
bushes after all," said Upshaw, pointing to the iridescent shapes
that their camera's telephoto lens revealed to be bushes for sure.

"That thing in the roof? That's a fucking antenna," exclaimed
Dr. Garibaldi. "Looks like a jumbo version of the patch antennas
inside our cell phones."

"Think it's picking up signals from far away?"

"Bet on it."

"I dunno," cautioned Holzgraf. "our radio and the spectrum
analyzer did not see a thing."

"Well, that's easy — they're not transmitting. Just listening."

"Who? Who is listening? And, more important, listening to
what?" wondered Upshaw. "Disco music? Letters from loved
ones? Or . . . orders?"

Garibaldi backed out of the huddle. He clasped hands, cracked
his knuckles. "Orders, instructions. Sounds right."

▼

General Congreve was not pleased to hear the ITF report.

"Jesus Christ, Mo. We were all over Arizona with a microscope. Satellites, aircraft, sensors in every mode you ever heard of. We could see ants on the ground. How did this happen?"

"Don't know, Russ. When did Wild Harvest last sweep through here? Couple of years ago, according to the report I'm reading."

"We sanitized the hell out of Tucson. And the rest of the world too, don't forget."

"Clearly, you missed something. I'm not gloating — maybe my team missed something too. Now, we've got worries a lot bigger than ants."

▼

Two huge CH-47 twin-rotor Chinook helicopters descended without warning onto an asphalt pad at the Paloma Valley regional airport just outside Marana. Flight school instructors and Air National Guard crews dropped their logbooks and tools and rushed outside to watch the choppers disgorge four Army personnel carriers and a platoon of heavily armed soldiers. They gawked as the soldiers boarded the vehicles and tore away into the western desert on Paloma Valley Road.

Less than half an hour later a C-130 Hercules cargo airplane made a landing on the main runway. Trucks, trailers, and Humvees emerged from the hold. They raced away in the same direction as the personnel carriers.

Airport workers were perplexed. Some shook their heads in wonderment and returned to their jobs, others ran for their cars and eagerly followed the military vehicles.

By the time civilian observers reached the scene, construction engineers were busy stringing razor wire along the top of the chain link fence surrounding Aztec Rubber Recovery. Once that task was completed, they spent a few minutes pounding stakes equipped with motion sensors into the hard caliche soil at ten-yard intervals.

A squad of soldiers armed with tasers and M-16s began patrolling the newly erected perimeter. The rest of the detachment stood back to await events.

The ITF team arrived just as the situation stabilized. Holzgraf and Chow brought three handmade prototypes of their microwave guns with them.

"Not quite up to production standards, you understand," said Holzgraf as he handed them off to the detachment's commanding officer, one Captain Hugh Donaldson.

"But they should be effective," insisted Chow as she ran through the details of their operation. "Any strangers we don't like, we can dissolve with these things."

The captain was dubious, but the prospect of an alien presence with unknown powers had all the soldiers on edge, and they grasped the weapons like life preservers.

Upshaw checked his watch. "Any action? Movement? I don't see any activity."

Donaldson shook his head. "Place seems deserted, sir. Unless you credit my radio man, here. He thinks he saw someone standing in that open doorway when we first arrived."

Within the hour a Blackhawk helicopter appeared overhead. It circled the tire recycling property, found an open spot behind the accumulated military equipment, and landed. General Congreve appeared in the doorway. He put on a pair of sunglasses, jumped down onto the ground, and headed for the operation perimeter. He was followed by a young man in a suit and tie. They worked through the mesquite bushes, wove their way between the military vehicles, and approached the ITF group. Congreve spent a moment silently studying the rusty metal building and the pile of tire carcasses. He was unimpressed.

"Whatcha got, Mo? Why am I here?"

"The employees of this company have all been reported missing by their families. We spotted conclusive evidence here of the bushes Wild Harvest was supposed to have eradicated."

"Where are they? Show me these bushes."

"On the other side. They're growing. We think the missing employees have been transformed. We think they're in communication with the visitors' home planet."

Congreve was about to protest, but at that moment a creature issued from the building, moving lightly on many legs. It took a few steps toward the observers, then retreated back inside; an undeniably alien being of unknown heritage, uncomfortably strange.

"One of them?" asked Congreve.

"What else?" muttered Upshaw, shrugging off a sudden chill.

Garibaldi showed the general a composite picture of the missing men, assembled from their driver license photos. "We were hoping for something more like these people, more like Florencio Rojas, whose car was seen during the DM break-in we reported."

Congreve nodded grimly. "All right, I get it. Mo? What do you think? Recommendation?"

Upshaw scratched his balding head. "Watch and wait?"

The young man in the suit and tie pointed a finger. "Who's that?" he asked.

A figure was striding toward them.

"Good Lord," said Upshaw. "That looks a lot like Jim."

Chow bounced up and down. "See? I told you I saw him!"

The figure stopped walking just inside the perimeter. Soldiers, primed for scary surprises, tightened their grip on their weapons. But whoever or whatever it was did not seem alien at all, just a man, a well-favored anglo at that, dressed in jeans and a dusty sweatshirt. He touched a finger to the razor wire. He smiled sardonically.

"General Upshaw," he called out.

"Rojas?" wondered Congreve.

Upshaw ignored the question and edged forward to the perimeter. "Jim, that you?"

Captain Donaldson joined him with a video camera running.

The man wrinkled his brow and spread his hands. "Used to be." The voice was loud and unmodulated, impersonal.

"Yes, well, it's been a while," agreed Upshaw. "Good to see you up and on your feet. We thought . . ."

". . . you thought I was dead."

Upshaw grimaced. "Yes we did. Suicide, right in front of the team. An unexpected revelation."

The man nodded.

"That was then. Now I'm what you might call an emissary. A representative for my fellow visitors, whose English is not so good. And I bring a message: tell your military pals to keep their powder dry, okay? We're not hurting anyone."

"Well, Jim, let's look at the situation. Who have you got in there? Where are the Aztec employees?"

"They're here, working with us."

"I've got to ask — are they still human?"

The man's eyes seemed to go blank. He blinked. He drew himself up. "Human? With human frailties? Poverty? Helpless anger? No, not that kind of human. They're much better off now. Well taken care of. Potentially immortal."

"Your own transformation, as I understand it, took years. These men were recently reported missing by their families. All of a sudden they're robots. What's the story?"

The erstwhile army officer stuck his chin out. "This is different, different technique, that's all."

Upshaw and Captain Donaldson exchanged looks with eyebrows raised.

"Right. That sounds encouraging, I guess," ventured Upshaw. "I'm just an emissary myself, Jim. We need to talk among ourselves, you understand?"

"Of course."

"You know, how to establish relations going forward. You and your *visitors* — unprecedented. Nothing like this has ever happened before."

"We await your deliberations."

Upshaw backed away from the perimeter and trudged back toward the rest of his colleagues, motioning Donaldson to follow.

The former Jim Lockwood remained where he was standing, apparently inert.

▼

The human brain trust gathered in a trailer General Congreve had set up as a command post.

"So, ladies and gentlemen, what do we do?"

"Live and let live," said the young man in the suit and tie. "We should acknowledge a proper delegation from another country, behave like civilized people."

"Excuse me," said Upshaw. "Who are you?"

"Sorry, everyone," said Congreve. "Say hello to Bernard Wyatt. He's a deputy national security advisor to the President."

The rest of the group focused on the young man.

"Call me Barney."

"All right, Barney," said Garibaldi, "we've got an alien invasion going on here. Arrivals in secret, practicing stealth. No advance notice."

"Invasion? How many aliens, Doctor?" rejoined Wyatt, not in the least intimidated by the ITF scientist.

"An infestation, then, how's that?"

Wyatt grinned. He was enjoying the beginnings of a debate. "Something new, for sure," he granted. "First time in human history, right? And I can tell you that the President will want these things — beings, entities, aliens, whatever — contained. So we agree on that. But not harmed."

Weatherall wasn't convinced. "Two guards at Davis-Monthan were killed to recover Lockwood's ingredients, if that's what the sand we archived really is. Four more people have been transformed as well — or duplicated and disposed of. So your friendly visitors have committed six murders so far."

"I didn't say they were friendly," protested Wyatt. "Just due a thoughtful measure of respect."

"By their standards we're primitive and therefore vulnerable," worried Garibaldi. "Remember — Hernan Cortez conquered Mexico and wiped out an entire civilization with a hundred men."

Holzgraf was equally uneasy. "What if they attack? Nobody mounts an expedition to cross sixty-five trillion miles of empty space just to say *hello.*"

Wyatt raised his hands, palms out, to fend off the doubts. "I don't pretend we know their intentions. And until we do, let's not provoke them into doing something we all might regret."

Upshaw nodded agreement. "We found them, we tied a knot on their activities. Let's keep a sharp eye out and see what develops."

Congreve was not optimistic. His military mind, previously anticipating some kind of police work, was starting to change as he surveyed the scene. "We have to assume our visitors are dangerous," he decided. "I think they are, maybe planning to kill us all. Right now we've got the upper hand. But they may have the means, given time, to reverse the balance of power. I vote we should burn everything to the ground and salt the earth underfoot."

"Whoa, General," cautioned Wyatt. "I'm here to prevent that, make sure the President is well served by his men in the field."

Upshaw frowned. "Look at you. How old are you? How long in your job? How do we know that you really represent the President's views?"

Wyatt reddened, stung by the challenge. He produced a satellite phone and pressed a key. "Hello, Betty? Put the Man on the phone, please."

Pause.

"I don't care if he's screwing his wife as we speak. This is urgent."

Pause.

"Hello, Mr. President. As you anticipated, we have a range of opinion on handling the visitors we've discovered out here in Arizona. Care to clarify for the team? Your voice will calm the waters."

Pause.

Wyatt listened briefly and handed the phone to General Congreve.

"Mr. President," said the mission commander, flattered by the attention. He listened for a moment, then yanked the phone away from his ear. Everyone in the trailer could hear the President shouting from the other end of the call.

"Got it, sir. Don't worry, will do."

He handed the phone back to Wyatt and addressed the group.

"Barney called it, and the President confirms. For the moment, we do nothing."

7

WHILE HUMAN authorities discussed their options, the alien spider-like creature, previously only glimpsed, crept out of the tire shop and advanced on the perimeter fence. It raised its front legs above the razor wire. White-hot plasma beams shot forth from its claws, slicing through the wire and the fence underneath. It grappled with the collapsing chain link, thrust it aside, and moved slowly and deliberately toward Captain Donaldson, who was standing guard nearby.

"Hey, there," the Army man shouted to the former James Lockwood, also nearby, standing guard for the other side. "Yes, you! Call off your pet!"

Lockwood either didn't hear or ignored the command, and the spider-like creature continued toward Donaldson, who backpedaled into the scrub, where he tripped over a small cholla.

The spider-like creature stood over him, front legs poised to strike. Donaldson desperately raised Holzgraf and Chow's prototype microwave weapon, found the switch, turned it on, and pressed the trigger with a shaky finger. A laser dot appeared on his possible assailant.

Lockwood roused himself when he heard the high-pitched whine of the weapon revving up for battle. "Don't shoot! He's harmless! Hold your fire!"

Too late. Donaldson pressed the trigger with greater force. The weapon caught the spider-like creature in its beam. The thing shuddered and, like a dog shaking itself off after a swim, threw off clouds of sparkling particles before dissolving completely into a pile of sand.

Lockwood rushed toward the Army man. "You fool!" he barked. Donaldson thought he was going to be attacked. In a panic he pressed the weapon's trigger a second time.

"Noooo!"

Lockwood threw up his hands. Clouds of particles floated from his head and arms. He collapsed.

Donaldson struggled to his feet and moved to examine the results of his actions. Lockwood no longer existed. His clothes lay in a crumpled pile with opalescent sand spilling from his sleeves and pant legs.

"Oh my God."

Donaldson lifted a small walkie-talkie from his belt and pressed the transmit button.

"General? You better get out here. I might have made a tactical mistake."

General Congreve and his group were quick to respond. But before they could reach the perimeter, two cars and a pickup truck erupted from the building, shot through the hole in the perimeter fence, and blazed away through the mesquite. One of them towed a battered section of chain link fencing several hundred yards before it tore loose.

Upshaw noted a line of dust rising behind the receding vehicles.

"Get a chopper up there, pronto. Follow those cars!"

But scrambling the only available helicopter proved tedious. The pilot was in the porta potty just then, and when he did emerge he was forced to warm up the engine for several minutes before all his gauges signaled flight readiness.

"Shit, shit, shit," growled Congreve.

Upshaw was annoyed, but philosophic. "We'll find them. They left tracks."

Wyatt was furious. "We better. We may have to apologize." He toed Lockwood's pants, spilling more of the former human's sandy remains. "Look at this! Humanity's first fucking encounter, and how did we comport ourselves? By causing a fucking fatality! How does that make us look, huh? Like animals!"

"Lockwood was dead already, Barney. Three years ago."

"Yeah? The man looked pretty spry to me. That blows our dip-lomatic relations, and my job is on the line."

▼

Once the group calmed down, they mounted a reconnaissance foray into the abandoned recycling plant. They made note of a large rectangular excavation in the floor and oohed and ahhed over a gleaming machine the size of a large delivery van. It was attached to the antenna sticking up through the roof, its purpose unknown. Even as they watched, it began to dissolve.

"It's melting," said Chow, "just like the Wicked Witch of the West."

Sure enough, within a few minutes the antenna and the ma-chine were reduced to a mound of glassy particles, apparently the same material that once constituted James Lockwood.

"What was going on here?" wondered Weatherall. "Not much of a hideout, really."

Garibaldi pointed at his smartphone.

"See — I took this picture just before the whatever-it-was started to dissolve. Look over here — an intake port?" He touched the screen. "And here, a large opening where something inside could pop out."

"Why the hole?" wondered Holzgraf.

"Maybe the dirt was . . . raw material," speculated Chow.

"You think they were manufacturing something?"

"Maybe so. Probably not tires, though."

▼

As night fell across the desert and turned Aztec Rubber Recovery into a cluster of indistinct shapes, Congreve ordered his men to continue patrolling the abandoned facility at full strength.

"Don't know what's going on, what might happen. Eyes wide."

The soldiers involved were jumpy and irritated. Also cold and hungry, factors that helped establish a surly mood. Either their vigilance was ridiculously useless, or they were being set up as early-warning targets.

But nothing untoward happened far into the night. The ITF team assisted their military colleagues in collecting the alien bushes growing beside the building. They gathered up quantities of otherworldly sand. They stored their collection in an Army truck and locked it up tight.

The Moon set at midnight, and by oh-dark-hundred the soldier standing guard at the missing section of chain link fence began to let his thoughts drift. Included in his reverie was the sound of a motor vehicle. Except the sound, although faint, was real.

Suddenly a Polaris Scrambler quadricycle leaped out of the desert scrub, headlight off. It collided with the guard, knocking him into the pile of tire carcasses. The driver continued on to the point where Lockwood was dissolved and dismounted with a black light playing over the ground. Here and there the purplish beam picked up glowing bits of sand. The driver scooped them into a plastic bag, remounted his quad, and blasted back into the night.

The rest of the patrol gathered around their fallen comrade, but they were too late to stop the intrusion. The ITF contingent was sorely disappointed, and General Congreve was sorely pissed.

8

NICOLETTE TRAEGER, a handsome, energetic, willowy woman of forty years, was the seasoned nightly anchor on KTVK, the major TV news channel in Phoenix, Arizona. She was noted for her no-nonsense approach to the stories she told, and for her lightly bemused attitude toward the fires, car crashes, and convenience store robberies that filled most of her on-air hours. Station management liked her professionalism and her easy way with happy talk, as did the station's audience: her show was the highest rated eleven-o'clock news program in the state.

Traeger was not entirely comfortable with her situation, however. She began her career as an investigative reporter, following grim stories in Latin America, the Middle East, and the darker side of life in the United States, writing up the wrongs of the world for various online media outlets. After years of marginal living and a series of failed grant proposals, she discovered that her appetite for the news could be satisfied on television at a very good salary. She was glad of the comfort, but itching for action.

Today, planning for the evening show found her in a huddle with her editorial assistant Julia Maxwell, with whom she had occasionally shared a bed. Something was going on down in Tucson.

"Look, Nikki, the *Star* had this piece on page 3 yesterday:

POLICE ACTION IN MARANA

Tire recyclers breaking the rules, or drug dealers breaking the law? Many questions and few answers hover over this incident at a tire recycling plant out in the unpopulated desert west of Tucson's suburban settlements.

Traeger frowned. "Yeah, what?"
Maxwell opened a web page on her laptop.

"Here's a clip from KVOA. They covered the story from their helicopter."

From an oblique point of view circling the action a quarter mile away, grainy video of the Aztec Rubber Recovery plant was visible on Maxwell's screen. Military vehicles could be seen parked nearby. Soldiers could be seen on patrol.

"Well now," said Traeger, "that's some police action."

"Exactly. ICE and DEA, they have white trucks, they usually wear civvies and those windbreaker jackets. The men here — soldiers in full combat dress. Plus, their vehicles — camo paint — and I count at least three heavy-duty personnel carriers."

"Unh-huh. The Force is with them."

"You're not kidding. So — question — what is the military doing down in Marana?"

"They're not fighting enemy tires, that's for sure."

"No ma'am. Big immigration bust, you think? Why the Feds? Why so secret?" Maxwell wriggled around in her chair, imagining exciting scenarios. "Maybe it's something weird, huh? We don't know."

"No, we don't."

"This is your kind of stuff, Nikk. Want to pick it up tonight?"

Traeger was intrigued. She thought about the idea. "No, there's another shoe that needs to drop. And we don't know enough to drop it."

"Mmm."

"I know, this looks juicy to you, but the cake isn't even half-baked. Stay with it, maybe we'll know more in a day or two."

"All right. So instead, we go with the latest drought news? Hey, you can predict the date when our temp first tops one-hundred-degrees."

"Don't gripe, Jules. If the police gig turns out to be important, I will yell from the rooftops."

9

TRAEGER WAS nothing if not inquisitive. Between editorial meetings and wardrobe fittings, she started checking news stories from all over the Southwest, looking for more pieces to Maxwell's jigsaw puzzle.

She found one in a follow-up story to the Tucson *Daily Star's* first notice of the "police action" in Marana. Four employees of the tire recycling plant had been reported missing. She thought that was odd.

Another piece of the puzzle turned up in a police report Maxwell dug out of the Maricopa County sheriff's office in Avondale using KTVK's professional search tools.

"Five more people missing, Nikki. Some grimy wrecking yard out near Wintersburg. Undocumented Hispanics, probably. They went to work one day and never returned home."

Traeger nodded absently. She was leafing through the back pages of yesterday's *Arizona Republic.*

"Hey, Jules — Wintersburg is just up the road from the big atomic plant, right?"

"Yes, that's the mailing address."

"Have a look at this . . ."

PALO VERDE BROWNOUTS

Arizona residents have new cause for concern regarding the safety and efficiency of the largest nuclear power plant currently operating in the entire United States, which has experienced a series of brownouts in the past 72 hours.

Plant operators seem as baffled by the problem as the puzzled residents of Tonopah and Glendale, where lights have been dimming unpredictably for more than a month.

Traeger drummed her fingers on her desk. "That plant — it's a star, America's poster child for safe, successful, reliable nuclear power. I have never heard of a brownout."

Maxwell cocked her head. "And . . . what? I don't see the connection."

Traeger grinned. "I don't either." Her brow wrinkled with suspicion. "But I'm betting we've got one. Big atomic plant, the military, missing persons . . . "

"I could find some B-roll of the power plant," said Maxwell. "We could talk about the safety angle. People are scared to death of anything nuclear."

Traeger lifted a finger. "No, call Teddy."

Maxwell pouted playfully. "My rival?"

"He's just a guy, Jules. I want to get a good look. Make sure he's got a camera with him."

▼

KTVK's Eye-In-The-Sky, a Bell JetRanger helicopter decorated in flashy brown and yellow trim with a giant Channel 3 logo on the door, flew westward away from the urban sprawl of metropolitan Phoenix and out into the bald desert. Ted Purley, the contracting pilot, and Nikki Traeger, his passenger and occasional lover, had their headsets on against the howl of the engine and the beat of the blades.

"I can't fly right over Palo Verde, Nikk. Restricted airspace."

"I know, get close. Put the Sun at about ninety degrees, and I'll capture some radioactive footage."

Purley nodded. He aimed the bird toward Wintersburg.

"You know, that assistant of yours — she was pretty crisp when she called me."

"Unh-huh, she's just jealous."

Purley was a good-looking guy and proud of his masculinity. Before he signed up to ferry newshounds studying rush hour traffic patterns, he served in Afghanistan ferrying wounded soldiers to hospital units. That's where he first met Traeger, the intrepid reporter. He raised his eyebrows.

"I've heard the rumors, babe. So, tell me — you swing both ways?"

Traeger touched his shoulder affectionately. "Brave in all things, Teddy. Brave in all things."

He chuckled drily, brave enough himself to accept the situation.

They flew on in silence. Forty miles out of the city, the buildings and roads of Maricopa County thinned out and the Palo Verde Nuclear Generating Station came into view. Three gigantic concrete mushrooms housed three reactor cores set among auxiliary structures, cooling towers, an electrical transmission switchyard, and a vast checkerboard of ponds that cooled the reactors with treated sewage.

Purley steered his JetRanger to the north and slowed to a walking pace, placing the Sun on his right and establishing the plant in oblique light and shadows that emphasized its solid immensity. Traeger aimed the video camera and spent a few minutes recording the location from a slowly changing point of view.

"Don't see anything that might indicate trouble. You?"

"No crews running around, no trucks."

Purley fiddled with a radio.

"Nothing on my scanner. We'd hear plenty of chatter if something was wrong."

Traeger put the camera away.

"Yeah, shit, it would be nice to get the scoop on some terrible accident, leakage, radioactivity contaminating the mesquite for miles around."

Purley raised a hand. He punched a button to rescan a range of radio frequencies.

"Hey — got something — listen to this . . ."

Traeger bent forward, clapped hands over her headset to drown out any residual chopper noise.

"All I hear is squelch."

"Wait, wait . . . now — !"

Voices rose above the background noise. Commands that weren't quite clear were being issued and acknowledged.

"Okay, that's something. Cops? What are they doing out here?"

"Not cops. Not their radio band."

Traeger glanced around at the empty territory. She pointed northwest to a line of extinct volcanic mounds.

"What's behind those hills? Let's get over there."

Purley nodded. He made a pedal turn, levered his cyclic pitch control, and put the JetRanger into forward motion.

Soon they rounded the nearest hill flanking the Stone Valley area of rural Tonopah. What they saw in the hollow below was an automobile wrecking yard. Acres upon acres of derelict cars and trucks sprawled around the oval bulk of a rusting Quonset hut that had once been painted white. The letters SVS&S were scrawled over the curving roof.

The place looked deserted, except for the military vehicles parked to one side and soldiers patrolling the rickety chain link fence that marked the yard's boundary. Traeger counted a dozen personnel carriers. Purley pointed to three Blackhawk helicopters on the ground. As they flew closer they saw a big cargo chopper slowly descend on the scene and deposit a portable building the size of a large recreation vehicle.

"Field latrine," noted Purley.

"Oh my God, do I see a *tank?* Yes — more than one!" exclaimed Traeger.

Sure enough, three tank-like vehicles were strategically positioned to fire on the Quonset hut if so ordered. More soldiers came into view. Some were digging trenches, others were arranging sandbags around machine gun emplacements.

"Holy crap, Ted! This can't be a drug bust. Can't be immigrant bullshit."

"Maybe they got one of those cults. You know, some old patriarch hiding out with a dozen wives."

"Like Waco, back in the day. But with heavy artillery."

"Sure, why not?"

Traeger snorted. "Does this look like an FBI operation to you?"

Purley shook his head. "Not really."

At that moment a loud radio voice interrupted their speculations with an order.

"You in the chopper! Channel 3! This is a military operation, and you are violating secure airspace. Depart immediately!"

Purley held course.

"Right, don't listen, they can't shoot us."

The voice barked a contradictory warning. "No Fly Zone! Depart immediately! We are authorized to shoot if you fail to comply."

Purley veered away. Traeger aimed the video camera at the wrecking yard and recorded the location as it swiveled away behind them.

"I'm not leaving, Ted. Put me down somewhere. I'm going in there."

"Are you nuts?"

"What? Think they'll arrest me?"

"I think your station will fire my ass if I let you do it."

"Ain't gonna happen. I have veto power."

Purley mulled the situation.

"It's a long walk home, babe."

"So I'll bum a ride. Hah — from them!"

Purley lowered his machine onto a barely visible gravel track snaking through mesquite bushes, chollas, and prickly pear cacti.

Traeger jumped out, latched the helicopter's door, gave it a thump, and Purley pulled up and away. Traeger shielded her eyes from the dust raised by the rotors' downdraft. She judged the wrecking yard was less than half a mile away. She started walking in what she hoped was the right direction.

Pretty soon she was moving past the rusted hulks of cars from bygone days. Here an old Studebaker, there a Kaiser. When the Quonset hut came into view she made a point of shooting snippets of video with her smartphone camera. Among the images she captured were a helicopter dangling a Humvee on a long cable, a couple of cannons being wheeled into position, and a squad of soldiers in full combat gear.

A few hundred yards short of the almost solid expanse of abandoned sheet metal, a cloud of dust heralded a jeep roaring toward her. She slipped her smartphone into her right boot. The jeep skidded to a stop, blocking her way. A soldier stepped out and confronted her. He was carrying an M-16 rifle with his finger poised along the trigger guard.

"Ma'am, you are trespassing on a military operation."

"Calm down, soldier. I'm a journalist — KTVK — and you are a story."

"Don't tell me to calm down, ma'am. This area is dangerous, and it is off-limits to civilians. Get in the jeep."

Traeger reached into a pocket and brought forth a second smartphone. She commenced to record video.

"We've got a free press, soldier. And I am curious — what the fuck are you doing out here?"

The soldier reached out, grabbed her phone, dropped it on the hard ground, and crushed it underfoot.

"Get in the jeep. *Now.*"

10

TRAEGER WAS exhilarated by her afternoon foray. Her professional associates were not.

"Ted told us you were out there, risking your hide, risking your show," admonished her supervisor. "The operation you discovered is secret — what if the Army disappeared you into some detention center, never to be heard from again?"

"Hey, I'm here."

"Yeah, you got away with it. You're a valuable asset, Nikki, and we've invested a lot of money in you. Any more episodes like this and I'll have to invoke breach of contract."

Traeger grinned. "It's a good story, right? You're not going to kill it?"

The KTVK boss was angry, but he couldn't help admiring Traeger's initiative. "Fill in the details. Make it quick. By tomorrow I may see some damn court order to cease and desist."

▼

Traeger recounted her escapade while she and Maxwell did some fact checking.

"So the creep in the jeep drove me up to Salome Road. I had to hike a couple of miles before I hitched a ride with some woman from the nuclear plant whose shift just ended."

Missing the big adventure put Maxwell in a surly mood. "What about brownouts? She say anything?"

"Not a word. I should have quizzed her."

"Well, okay, but while you were farting around out there I spotted an email exchange between the mayor of Glendale and plant management. Palo Verde will not admit to any brownouts. They don't see a problem. But Tonopah, Wintersburg, and Dixie Park, they all report them."

"Get anything off my personal phone the guy smashed?"

"The lab managed to tease out one still photo. Your chauffeur."

"Is it presentable? On the air?"

Maxwell brightened. The prospect of a big scoop was intoxicating. "Oh my God, yes. That, the video from your other phone, footage from the chopper. Wow. We just have to write the narrative to string this stuff together."

"We've got two hours. Order some pizza, willya?"

▼

The KTVK eleven o'clock news show began with supergraphics splashed across TV screens all over Arizona:

BREAKING NEWS
BREAKING NEWS
BREAKING NEWS

Traeger appeared behind her desk. She was wearing glasses and staring at her laptop. A pile of paper notes rested beside her. She referred to them as she laid out her tale.

"Hello, Arizona. Tonight we bring you a breaking story that's hot and getting hotter. Recently Tucson media reported on a quote — 'police action' — unquote, that took place on the outskirts of suburban Marana. Reporters in that city seemed to think the incident involved people seeking a better life here in the states, or if not, drug smugglers. But the so-called 'police action' did not involve ICE, or DEA or the Border Patrol. No, instead, the US Army was behind it all.

"Today I observed another 'police action' — ongoing as I speak — just west of the Palo Verde Nuclear Generating Station, our local power plant. Again the Army is running the show. Our research indicates that an ad-hoc unit called the *National Integrity Tactical Command,* known to insiders as *NITCOM,* has been marshalled to the area. A collection of special forces personnel, Rangers, SEALs, what have you, is in charge of the action, which looks to be targeting an auto wrecking yard called *Stone Valley Scrap & Salvage.*"

Photos and video clips taken by Traeger flashed onscreen.

"How serious is this?" she asked rhetorically. "The machine guns, tanks, armored personnel carriers, and soldiers you see on your TV screens prove that something big, something with dangerous potential, is going on. But what?"

Aerial footage of the atomic plant appeared. The lighting made the facility look dark and menacing.

"We also know that communities around Palo Verde have been reporting brownouts. Someone is stealing their power. A connection? We asked information officers at three different Army installations to comment, but they all refused. So we can't be sure, but it's an intriguing possibility.

"Even more intriguing is the disappearance of workers just a few weeks before these operations began. Nine people reported for work one day and have not been seen since. Four in Marana and five at the Stone Valley complex."

The camera panned away from Traeger to the station's late-night weatherman. "All is calm on a balmy evening here in Phoenix, folks, but I guess you think there's a storm brewing out west, Nikki, is that right?"

"Could be, Bert." Traeger removed her glasses and addressed the camera directly. "Speculation centers on action to curtail illegal immigration. With *tanks?* Maybe Stone Valley Scrap & Salvage is harboring undocumented aliens. The question in my mind is — where did they come from?"

"Good question, Nikki." The weatherman shivered theatrically. "We'll be back with tomorrow's chilly weather forecast right after this message from our sponsors . . ."

11

ON A LOW RISE a little to the southwest of Stone Valley
Scrap & Salvage, General Vernon Weaver, commanding officer
of the blandly named *Full Spectrum Threat Assessment Program,*
known to the few who had ever heard of it as *FULTAP,* joined
with General Upshaw to advise General Congreve on presumed
existential threats to NITCOM's present deployment in *Operation
Welcome Wagon.* They were sweating under a tent canopy with
an opening toward the wrecking yard that afforded a good view
of terrain they all thought might well become a battlefield.

"We're putting up razor wire, motion detectors . . . an armed
patrol is on duty. My best men. It's a measured response." Congreve sounded more confident than he felt.

"Down in Marana, some damn robot clipped that wire with
plasma torches embedded in its claws," noted Upshaw.

"How do we know we're looking at an alien infestation?" wondered Weaver. "Where's the proof?"

"Those bushes in Marana. And tracks," said Congreve. "We
followed an old pickup truck and a couple of quads from the first
go-around. They're here."

"Anywhere else? Russia? China?"

"No, we've been checking."

He handed Weaver a pair of binoculars.

The FULTAP commander gave the yard a quick survey.
"Okay, I see the hut, but no workers, no aliens. Just your men.
Looks like you're well set up."

"Will be," promised Congreve.

"All right then," said Weaver. "I don't know what you want
me around for."

Upshaw leaned against one of the posts supporting the canopy.
"No good reason, I guess. But we've had some interaction with

one of your agents. A young woman? Named Sarzeau? These things — aliens, robots, beings of some kind — we don't know the extent of their powers. What if they're telepathic, for example? Your people might be helpful."

Weaver put down the binoculars. He smiled. "You're talking about my girl, Marianne."

"Yeah, her. She helped us with those bushes. She's . . . unusual."

"Yes, very," said Weaver with a shake of his head. "There's no one else like her. She's good" — he made a thumbs up gesture — "but I don't think she's telepathic. Not a mind reader."

"Can we get her down here?"

"We can try. Gotta be careful, she's not a full-time agent, and she can be stubborn."

Congreve interrupted the discussion to point across the valley, where a Chinook helicopter was airlifting a large trailer into position.

"Here's my mobile command post, gentlemen. I believe it's air conditioned. Let's avail ourselves of the benefits of civilization" — he shrugged — "while we still can."

The three men moved quickly toward the trailer, then paused to watch it rotate on its wheelbase and expand crosswise, forming a wide office disguised by desert camo paint.

Inside, they gathered around a table, where a paper map assembled from Google Earth photos was spread out. It rustled under the blast from a powerful air conditioner.

Weaver pointed to green and blue stickers, placed at intervals around the perimeter of the wrecking yard image. "What — ?"

"Green are patrol pivot points, blue represent motion sensors. Those yellow dots to the side, there — tanks, cannon, machine gun emplacements."

"And the red ones?"

"Observed hostiles."

Weaver nodded. "Only seven instances?"

Congreve wiped his forehead with a tissue. "They're a sneaky bunch."

Soon they were distracted by the ripping snarl of an off-road quadricycle. It pulled up beside the command post and a very dusty Nicolette Traeger stepped off. She barely had time to brush her jeans and raise her goggles before three jeeps pulled up behind, beside, and in front of her. The soldiers aboard were yelling and swearing. One of them leaped off the nearest jeep and collared the news lady.

She did not resist, but flashed her TV credentials and demanded an audience with the man in charge.

▼

"And who are you? Reporter? TV anchor?" Congreve studied Traeger's ID. He was red in the face. "This is a classified operation, lady, and you have no business here. Nor will you be allowed to report on the situation. If you do not agree to cooperate, you will be detained. Am I understood?"

Traeger, whose right arm was firmly in the grip of a rugged soldier, lifted her chin. She glared at Congreve. "I already did."

"Did what?"

"Reported on your cover-up. The world wants to know what's going on, so I did my best to tell them. You and your operation here, you're news, General."

"Oh no we're not."

Upshaw smiled ironically and pointed out the window where several lines of dust proclaimed more vehicles arriving.

"Jesus Christ on a flaming taco!" growled Congreve.

Soldiers intercepted the SUVs, jeeps, dune buggies, quads, dirt bikes, and an ultralight airplane as they neared the command post and ordered the occupants out. Pretty soon a crowd of curious civilians had been herded into a tight group well back from the wrecking yard perimeter, surrounded by soldiers. They stared at the impressive military deployment with open mouths.

Congreve stared back. "How many of your faithful viewers found us, you think?"

"Quite a few, General," smiled Traeger impishly. "My show is popular. And I see another cloud of dust."

A big black Cadillac Escalade pulled up to the cluster of civilian vehicles and drove around them, horn honking. Irate soldiers waved them to a halt. The doors opened, and three men in suits emerged. They began arguing with their captors. Hands and arms were flailing. After a brief exchange, the lead soldier gave up and directed them toward the command post.

Bernard Wyatt climbed the steps to the trailer door, knocked politely, and let himself in.

"Barney," said Congreve. "You I know. Who's with you? I haven't had the pleasure."

"General, meet Secretary of State Morey Rutledge, and my boss, National Security Advisor Walter Melrose."

Congreve rocked back on his heels, then reached out to shake hands.

"Gentlemen," continued Wyatt, "this is Maurice Upshaw, who runs ITF, as we discussed, and here is Vernon Weaver, representing military intelligence." Wyatt didn't want to state the specific nature of FULTAP, a secretive arm of the Defense Department, because it specialized in psychic surveillance. He was worried that his very practical superiors would lose respect for the whole NIT-COM operation.

More handshakes. Congreve offered sparkling water from a built-in refrigerator.

Secretary Rutledge peered at the wrecking yard. He sipped his sparkling water. "I don't see anyone. No little green men."

Traeger overheard the man's remark. "Hah!" She slapped her thigh. "I knew it. What brings the fucking *Army* to town? *Aliens!*"

Congreve bristled. "Get her out of here!"

Traeger's non-com escort hustled her out of the command post. Rutledge waited to be sure she was out of earshot, then turned to Congreve.

"Sorry about identifying our targets. My mistake, but anything this big is bound to be noticed. I bring a message from the President, General. He wants — he is ordering you — not to take any action that would threaten our visitors. We have reached a unique moment in history, and we must not fumble the opportunity to properly greet the first beings ever to arrive from another world."

Congreve stiffened. "What if they come swarming out of their encampment with guns blazing?"

Rutledge tilted his head, thinking. "I seriously doubt that these creatures, having come a long way, through many hazards, want to start anything."

Upshaw took a step forward. "We've already experienced fatalities, Mr. Secretary — two air police at Davis-Monthan in Tucson, and another one, a soldier, during the Marana episode. There's a real danger."

"I hope for respect on both sides, and the President feels the same way." He shrugged. "Of course, in the unlikely event of an active threat, he allows for the reasonable application of defensive force."

National Security Advisor Melrose gestured toward the crowd outside. "I'm sorry that our containment effort here has been discovered." He grimaced. "Our free press is a pain in the ass. But you have to admire that woman's tenacity. Anyway you look at it, the cat is now out of the bag. The President will be forced to acknowledge the situation as it exists, and I think we need to revise our playbook."

Congreve blew out an irritated sigh. "Revise? How?"

Wyatt took up the torch. "May I suggest erecting a viewing platform where civilians can safely observe the field without getting in our way?"

Congreve gave his government visitors a sullen nod. "Where's Donaldson?"

Phase **2**

12

IN APPLEFIELD, California, a touristy village tucked into the foothills of the Sierra Nevada mountain range, the Sun was already up, although not yet visible over the imposing alpine heights.

In a loft-style house just off Main Street, Gabriel Sarzeau Wagstaff, a gangly seven-year-old second grader, was awake and restless. He threw the covers off his bed, stuffed his legs into a pair of jeans he was outgrowing, wiggled into a Yoda-themed T-shirt, and tiptoed out of his room to check on his parents.

Sleeping soundly nearby were Marianne Sarzeau, a local cop, and her husband, Tom Wagstaff. They were snuggled together in an elegant wooden bed handcrafted by Wagstaff himself as a courting gift before they were married.

Gabriel peered around the door frame to put an eye on the couple. Assured that they were actually asleep, he tiptoed into the kitchen, where he crammed crackers, M&Ms, and a box of apple juice into a Buzz Lightyear backpack.

Thus equipped, he eased out the front door and trotted off to the local park and the forest beyond.

Half an hour later Rachel, Gabriel's younger sister, crawled onto the Wagstaff marriage bed and wedged herself in between Mom and Dad. Her movements caused her parents to stir.

"Gabriel stole my M&Ms," she announced.

"Mmm," mumbled Sarzeau.

"And then he ran away."

Wagstaff rolled over. "Say what, sweetie? What did you say?"

"Gabriel ran away. I saw him."

Sarzeau sat up. She blinked away the fog of sleep. "What are you talking about, hon?"

"Gabriel ran away."

Sarzeau scowled. "Gabriel?" she called out, "Where are you? Get yourself in here!"

But Gabriel did not respond or materialize in their presence. Now the Wagstaffs were fully awake. They leaped out of bed and dashed down the hall for a look into their son's bedroom. Empty. Sarzeau ran through the house, shouting his name. Wagstaff ran outside in his underwear to scout the premises. They reconvened in the kitchen, both of them pale as ghosts and electrified with alarm.

"Where is he?" moaned Wagstaff. He ran an exasperated hand through his shaggy blond hair. "It's a school day, for crying out loud."

"I know. Wait. Wait a minute." Sarzeau slumped down on a kitchen stool and dropped her head into her hands. She started humming softly to herself.

Wagstaff observed his buxom young wife's peculiar behavior with concern, but also with considerable pride in knowing, without actually understanding, that she was tapping into one of her many uncanny abilities.

"Witchy stuff?" he asked.

Sarzeau held up a hand for silence. She began bobbing back and forth. Suddenly she jerked upright. She stood, ran back into the bedroom, and started throwing on her running gear.

"Gabe's on his way to the river. Somewhere on the Sluice Box Trail."

Wagstaff hastily donned T-shirt and shorts. He laced up his running shoes. "You saw him? You sure?"

"I didn't really see him. I felt him. Let's go! Go! We gotta go!"

"Oh shit. Rachel . . ."

"Rachel, honey? Go back to bed. We're going to get Gabe and your M&Ms. Can you do this? All by yourself?"

Rachel gave the idea some thought. "Yes, Mom," she said with an uncertain nod.

"We won't be long. Promise. So, bed. Sleep. Back soon."

Sarzeau kissed her child, Wagstaff carried her back to her bedroom, and the pair lighted out for the deep, dark, and largely pristine forest located in the uplands east of town.

They jogged through Applefield's picturesque park, past the bronze prospector statue, and into an overgrown field on a trail that led toward the woods. A quarter of a mile into the trees, they came to a hard choice where the trail split. One fork led down to the river, and the other up to Osprey Overlook, a local vantage point with views out across the foothills.

"Which way? Any idea?"

"*Nada . . .*"

Man and wife were both panting from their panicky run. Sarzeau fetched her phone from a pocket and punched a speed dial number,

"Damn. Better report this."

The local police office phone rang repeatedly before anyone picked up. But finally a voice wondered how to be of help to a good citizen of the Tri-Town area.

"Chief? That you? Oh, Rick! Hey, it's Marianne. This is embarrassing — my kid, Gabriel — he ran away just now. Up on the Sluice Box Trail, we think. We're up there now, but we haven't found him yet, so . . . we may need some help here."

The voice offered to requisition a police dog from Placerville to aid in the search. But now Wagstaff was waving frantically from a few yards along the trail leading down to the river.

"Hold that thought, Rick."

Sarzeau joined her husband, who lifted up a little red piece of lenticular candy between thumb and forefinger.

"Rachel's M&M?"

Sarzeau bent over, scanned the gravel at her feet, and found a similar piece of candy, this one yellow. She popped it into her mouth. "Gotta be. Where is that guy? I'm going to whale his little butt!"

They ran along the trail, down, down through woods clogged with bristling underbrush. Then, just around a massive granite outcrop that forced a sharp bend in the path, there was Gabriel, walking toward them, seemingly without a care.

"Hi, Mom," he said.

Sarzeau rushed forward with arms outstretched. She pulled her son into a big hug, lifted him high off the ground with a sigh of relief. Tears flowed. After a moment she handed him to Wagstaff, who administered another heartfelt hug.

"You! You are in deep shit, young man!" said Sarzeau, poking a finger in Gabriel's chest. "What do you think you were doing?! We were worried to death!"

Gabriel looked up at his parents, perplexed by their obvious anxiety.

"Whiskeyjack called me."

Sarzeau was thunderstruck. "Whiskeyjack . . ? He called you? Really, Gabe!"

Gabriel resented the doubts. "Yes he did. He's a bird. He gave me a present. It's for you."

The little boy handed over a small acorn.

"He wants to talk to you. He told me so."

▼

Back home, Sarzeau rolled the acorn around in her fingers, silently speculating what the gift might mean. It felt warm to the touch.

Many of her ancestors were known for their supernatural powers. Her father shared some of them, and Sarzeau herself was a late-blooming prodigy, what the serious books on witchcraft call an *adept*. She could sense the auras of other adepts; on occasion she could summon people; and she could sometimes command others to do her bidding. She could also cast the quaint old spells set forth in a book she received from her French cousins. Most impressive, to her and her loved ones, was her ability to see otherworldly creatures — ghosts and demons — that appeared in mirrors. Well, not all the time. Three years had gone by since she last made contact with a spirit who called himself Whiskeyjack.

Sarzeau led her family into the loft's master bathroom and stood in front of the wide mirror above a pair of sinks.

"Okay, boys and girls. Watch carefully, you might or might not see anything."

Tom Wagstaff was a well-educated, thoughtful, but otherwise ordinary human, who had learned to accept his wife's extraordinary talents. He took up a hopeful position behind his son and daughter. Once, years before, he got a glimpse of something blurry in a mirror. He was always on the lookout for a better view.

Sarzeau reached under her shirt and withdrew a small stone on a leather necklace, an amulet chipped from a rocky enclosure on the coast of France. She gripped it tightly in one hand while she fingered the acorn in the other.

"Whiskeyjack," she whispered. "You there? It's Marianne."

They waited for a while, but nothing seemed to happen. At times like these, Sarzeau resorted to a cruder approach.

"Hey you!" she shouted, startling her kids. "Earth calling Whiskeyjack! Listen up over there!"

Again, nothing. But after a few seconds the room seemed to darken. A smoky cloud intruded on the family's image in the mirror. It boiled outward. A pair of electric blue eyes broke through the cloud.

Marianne. It is good to see you whole and well.

The sonorous voice was entirely in Sarzeau's head. She nodded. "Same here, old pal. Tell me, why are you talking to my son? He's just a kid. You scared us half to death."

I called, but you didn't hear me. Hence the acorn to help attune your thoughts.

"Okay, I'm tuned. What's up in spiritland?"

Important news that cannot wait.

"Uh-oh. I don't like the sound of that."

Nor should you. Creatures from far away have arrived on your world.

"Really? Men from Mars?"

They are mechanical, the product of other beings' skill. They did not grow and evolve, so they have no feelings, no friends, no scruples, no sympathies. That makes them unpredictable.

"Oh boy . . ."

You must go to them, help your people discover their intentions. Welcome them, or fight them if necessary.

"Where? Why me?"

You will see things others overlook. In the desert.

"Arizona? Those crazy bushes? I did this already."

Now they are creatures. Shaped from crystals. You must go.

"Can't my father take care of this? I'm raising a family here."

Blue eyes blazed.

Take Gabriel with you. I foresee a role for him to play.

Before Sarzeau could utter another objection, the eyes winked out. The smoky cloud withered and vanished.

Sarzeau slumped against the countertop. She was pale and shaking. Suddenly she leaned over and vomited into the sink.

Tom took her into his arms.

"Hey, babe, you okay?"

Sarzeau wiped her mouth on a towel. "Urrrr . . ." she said. "Holy crap, I hate these encounters."

Wagstaff and the children looked at each other, looked at wife and mom with inquiring stares.

"What — ?"

"You were talking to yourself."

"Oh no, guys. That was real. Didn't you see him?"

Wagstaff shrugged. "The lights seemed to dim. I'm telling myself there was a blur."

Gabriel hopped up and down. "I saw him. He's not a bird. He's a cloud. He has big eyes!"

Sarzeau kissed her son on the top of his head.

"That's my boy."

Wagstaff returned from delivering Gabriel to school and found his wife searching frantically through drawers and cupboards.

"Whatcha need, babe?"

Sarzeau blew a strand of hair out of her eyes. "My secure phone."

Wagstaff moved to the office where he wrote and edited the Tri-Town area's local newspaper, the *Amador County Courier.* He unlocked a small safe underneath his desk and handed a bulky satellite phone to his wife.

Now and then Sarzeau's job as a local police officer was overshadowed by her alternate role as a federal agent for the Defense Department's mysterious FULTAP outfit, which employed her powers to deter evil plots and schemes. Her father was also an agent, and she was recruited to stand in when, years ago, he was trapped in a supernaturally induced coma.

She punched a number into her phone.

"Hi there, Full-of-Crap. Sarzeau *femme* on this end. I'd like to speak to Agent Scanner or Ray Bagwell, please."

Pause.

"Okay, put him on."

Pause.

"General Weaver. Good to hear your voice. I just got wind of something going on down in Arizona, and one of my spooky contacts urged me to get myself down there."

Pause.

"That's right — really spooky. Know anything about this?"

Pause.

"Oh, you're already there. Outside Phoenix. Where's Dad? Where's Ray?"

Pause.

"Classified. Right. Okay then, looks like I'm coming off the bench. See you soon."

She put the phone down on Wagstaff's desk. She was lost in thought.

"Well?" Wagstaff arched his eyebrows. "What's the good news . . . *Broomer?*"

"Those bushes I got involved with back when? Now they've turned into creatures. A number of people have been killed. Some have been transformed."

Wagstaff slapped his forehead. "Fucking *aliens.*"

"Them from there, for sure. Dad is off somewhere on another project, and FULTAP wants me on the scene, pronto."

"Wow, this is history."

"I guess."

"You bet it is. And you'll be part of it. But, hey, you don't look too excited by the idea."

"It's going to be dangerous. Maybe they have death rays or who knows what. And Whiskeyjack wants Gabriel to be there too. He thinks it's important."

Wagstaff's enthusiasm melted away. "You didn't mention that."

"No, but he made a point of telling me — Gabriel figures into this somehow."

"How does your blurry demon pal know that?"

Sarzeau looked at her husband through narrowed eyes. "As you may remember from many earlier conversations, dear — I don't understand almost anything I know how to do."

Wagstaff stomped around his office, waving his arms.

"Well, if you're taking Gabe, you're also taking me."

"No way — someone has to watch Rachel."

"Make that my mother. I may not be able to read monster minds, but I'm a journalist, and this is the biggest story since the biblical flood."

13

FORTY-EIGHT HOURS after KTVK broke the news, hundreds of people had already gathered at the Stone Valley Scrap & Salvage facility to witness the first contact between humans and beings from another planet. More were arriving in a steady stream. Roads to the site through Tonopah, Wintersburg, and Hassayampa were clogged with traffic.

Ted Purley was overhead again in the KTVK helicopter, recording the traffic jams.

Nikki Traeger was on camera beside the newly erected visitor platform with the latest news and gossip.

Into this swarm of people and vehicles came Holly Chow and Guy Holzgraf. They were late to the party, but managed to beat the traffic by flying up from Tucson in Holzgraf's little Robinson helicopter.

"Oh my God," wailed Chow, "look at this crowd. We need another viewing stand."

"Make that two or three, and set them a long way back, you ask me," grudged Holzgraf.

Chow scowled. "Yeah, if Congreve's meet and greet goes south, we could see a lot of casualties."

After talking their way past the sergeant on duty as a traffic cop, they presented the latest prototype microwave weapon to Congreve and Upshaw.

"How many of these things have you got?"

"A dozen, all P2s — there's a P3 with a better battery, but otherwise we're ready for production. Let's hope we never get to use them."

Upshaw nodded. A young lieutenant took charge and moved off to distribute the weapons to the soldiers on patrol.

General Weaver's mobile phone rang. The voice on the other

end of the call caused him to glance out the window at an approaching OH-6 light observation helicopter in Army dress.

"Excuse me, folks."

He stepped outside and strode away to the landing area, where he greeted Marianne Sarzeau and family.

"Agent Broomhandle," said he. "And who is this?"

"Meet Tom Wagstaff, my husband. And this cute little kid — he's our son, Gabriel."

The general shook Wagstaff's hand and then, bending over to get an eye-level look, offered his hand to the little boy. "Hello, son," he said. "You here to look after your mother?"

"Yes I am, yup, for sure," replied Gabriel with unabashed confidence.

Weaver gestured toward the chaotic backdrop to the military operation. "No place for civilians, Broomer."

"We're not exactly civilians, Vern."

"Is Tom like you?"

"No."

"I'm a journalist, sir," explained Wagstaff. "Big story, don't you think?"

"And your boy . . ?"

Sarzeau nodded. "He's going to be something when he grows up."

"I better start recruiting, then. "You like ice cream, young fellow?"

Gabriel squirmed. "I guess so . . . chocolate chip mostly."

Weaver grinned. He pointed to a civilian concession stand some enterprising businessman had set up. "Got some for you. Right over here." He adjusted his hat. "Tom, sorry for the formality, break up the family so to speak, but — the press room is located over by the viewing stand. I can't invite you to join us up front here."

"Understood, General. See you later, M."

In the command post, General Congreve was outlining a surveillance mission to Captain Donaldson.

"I want you to take that drone right up over the top, get us photo coverage we can use to map this place. Then, drop down, give me a good shot of that open door, what they've got inside. Priority on any of the missing men that might be working for the red team."

"Got it, sir."

Donaldson picked up a radio transmitter, revved up a video drone the size of a pizza box, and sent it off over the wrecking yard.

The drone climbed a couple of hundred feet and stationed itself directly above the Stone Valley Scrap & Salvage Quonset hut. While the NITCOM brain trust watched the video output on Donaldson's laptop, Sarzeau reconnected with Chow and Holzgraf.

"The witch lady," remembered Chow. "And her child."

"Yeah, that's me. This is Gabe. Another me in the making."

Congreve turned toward the new arrival, taking notice of her rosy youth and curvy good looks. "A witch? Seriously?"

Sarzeau bobbed her head, tossing her ponytail around. "'Adept' is the word. I work for General Weaver. FULTAP."

"Hmm."

Sarzeau clocked the commander's frosty disbelief. "I'll try to help, only don't ask me to stop the invasion — if that's what this is — with a spell."

"Just don't turn me into a frog."

"She knows what she's doing, General," declared Holzgraf. "We've seen her in action."

Congreve paused. His brow wrinkled as he struggled to recall the details of a three-year-old mission briefing. "You know, I was told someone got a glimpse of the alien planet. Very woo-woo trick. Spotted robots, I think he said. That was you?"

Sarzeau made a little curtsy. "Yup. In a lucid dream."

Congreve gave her half a smile and held out his hand. She gave it a good shake.

"Got a name?"

"Marianne Sarzeau."

"Welcome to our circus, then."

Congreve gestured out the window to draw her attention to the hovering reconnaissance drone, NITCOM's current circus act. "Okay, Hugh, let's have a peek in that doorway."

Donaldson brought the drone down to within a few feet of the ground and moved it slowly around the side of the building to an open entrance wide enough to accommodate cars and trucks. The shadowy interior barely registered on his laptop.

"Don't see much. I'm going in," announced Donaldson. He tilted a control stick and the drone slowly advanced toward the interior of the Quonset hut.

Pffft

Suddenly, in the blink of an eye, the drone evaporated. A smoky cloud that marked its location drifted slowly away in the lazy air. The screen on Donaldson's laptop went dark.

"Well, damn," said Congreve.

Upshaw watched the event with one eye while he listened to a call on the command post's radio.

"Looks like they've got themselves some firepower," he observed. "And here's some more bad news, Russ. A forensic team has been going through the tire shop we raided down in Marana. I just got the report — they found bodies in the bottom of that hole we saw."

14

NOT LONG AFTER the drone incident, a figure emerged from the Quonset hut doorway and marched up to the perimeter fence. The figure looked an awful lot like James Lockwood, the erstwhile human.

He held up his arms in a broad gesture of greeting.

Doctors Weatherall and Garibaldi, hindered by the terrible traffic around Stone Valley, arrived at the NITCOM operation just in time to witness the figure's appearance.

"Well, look at that — Lockwood, or a very good imitation," said Garibaldi.

"Not dead — again! — how many lives does the man have?" wondered Weatherall.

"Nine? Like a cat?" suggested Chow.

"We're looking at a walking corpse, or an alien. Not a living human being, not Jim," growled Upshaw. "Hell, Jim worked for me for years, and this *creature* is something else. Doesn't walk like Jim, doesn't talk like Jim."

Captain Donaldson was on the command radio. He covered the mike with a hand.

"General Congreve? Patrol leader wants permission to dust this guy with one of our wavers."

Congreve scratched his nose. "Let's hear what he has to say, and then maybe we'll return their favor to our drone."

The Secretary of State stepped in between Donaldson and the commanding general.

"No, no, no. The President forbids any further bloodshed."

"There's no blood in that thing out there," countered Congreve.

"Nevertheless," insisted Rutledge, "no hostilities, except in the direst need for self-defense."

Congreve threw up his hands and turned toward the alien

version of Lockwood, who was climbing onto the wreck of an ancient Ford Falcon.

"Hello, people. I used to be one of you," said the figure, now standing high enough to be seen by everyone in the area. The voice was loud and on the tinny side, as if coming from a public address system.

"Some among you knew me well. ITF squad? I was part of it. Now I'm part of another group. Believe it or not, we have deep ties to Planet Earth. So, bring forth your reporters and your group leaders. Let's talk."

A troupe of reporters gathered and approached the perimeter fence with extreme caution, Nikki Traeger and Tom Wagstaff among them.

"We know you are debating among yourselves whether to eradicate us or not. Please don't assume we're hostile, bent on conquest."

Traeger elbowed her way to the front rank of the assembled journalists.

"How do we know anything about you?" she demanded. "You could be lying. You've heard of lies, I'll bet, right?"

The faux Lockwood held up a hand to call for a pause.

"Understandable concern. Why don't we let the leader of our expedition respond?"

At these words a silvery robot appeared in the Quonset hut doorway. It moved swiftly toward the group of journalists, floating on some sort of small hovercraft that kicked up a trail of dust.

"Ladies and gentlemen, let me introduce our guide and master, Director Brom-Kat-Su, in glorious fourth incarnation, with us today in body and spirit."

Traeger and Wagstaff exchanged doubtful glances.

"Glorious? Sounds like this guy is introducing a religious figure," whispered Wagstaff.

"Yeah, their pope maybe? I won't be kissing any rings, tell you that," grumbled Traeger.

Brom-Kat-Su, in glorious fourth incarnation, was large and imposing, but oddly shaped. He (if alien robots possessed the quality of gender) had no discernible head. No mouth. Four flexible limbs sprouted from a shiny slab of a torso. A row of black lenses, like spider eyes, circled around it.

"Hello, Earth dwellers," he said. His voice boomed from his body, as loud as the woofers in a teenager's hotrod automobile.

The crowd of journalists shrank back.

"The information to produce me came from another star," said Brom.

Inside the command post, Weatherall slapped a knee. "Those signals I told you about? Now we know what they were for."

"But I was born here on your planet," continued the robot, "while my other self remains at home. And although I look very different, and my stock is not like yours, we are cousins, made from the same elements lifted out of the ground."

Traeger snorted. This preposterous idea emboldened her to return to the perimeter fence, trailing her cameraman, who followed to record her brave advance.

"How cousins?" she asked. "Tell us why that's not impossible."

She thrust her microphone toward the robot.

Brom aimed one arm toward the desert floor and the other toward the sky.

"We are all alive — thinking, acting beings. That in itself unites us against the cold, empty, dead, uncaring universe."

15

THE SUN was going down behind the Eagletail mountains, twilight was fading, but the NITCOM and ITF leaders hardly noticed. They were embroiled in a long debate on the best way to handle their extraterrestrial visitors.

"No precedent. We've got nothing to go on," complained Secretary of State Rutledge.

"At least they can talk. They've been practicing. Very diplomatic show our old friend Lockwood put on, don't you think?" said Chow.

"Quite a vocabulary for a dead man," was Garibaldi's sour assessment. "And the robot too, Brom-what's-his-name."

"Let's remember where they came from, how hard it was to get here," said Weatherall.

"And why they bothered. That's the mystery," noted Upshaw.

Garibaldi was squinting out the command post window at the wrecking yard, where Congreve's brigade had encircled the area with powerful work lights.

"To repeat the obvious, no one — no one — sets off on a sixty-five *trillion* mile journey lasting a *century* to greet the neighbors. They want something. What do they want?"

National Security Advisor Melrose was drinking cold Army coffee. He swirled the liquid around in his cup. "Yes, what? What brought them to our doorstep? It's our job to find out. We can't act without knowing the answer to that question."

The debate droned on into the night without resolution. Eventually most of the conferees retired to bunks in an Army trailer.

Out on patrol, soldiers were on alert. They were all Rangers and SEALS, tough veterans of America's endless modern wars, and they were ready for anything.

Shortly after midnight, all the work lights winked out. Out of the blackened expanse of the wrecking yard what looked like a couple of Hispanic workmen popped up to confront Captain Donaldson, who was taking his turn on the line.

Donaldson staggered backward. He leveled his wave gun, and sprayed a desperate beam of microwaves at the duo. First one, then the other, dissolved into sandy piles.

At the same moment, from Donaldson's blind side, a glistening robot the size of a big dog ran up on spidery legs. It leaped on Donaldson, wrestled the wave gun out of his surprised fingers, and carried it away into the night.

16

IN THE MORNING, worried humans continued their alien containment discussion.

"They turned our lights out. How did they do that?"

"Forget the lights. They got a waver. They're analyzing it, how it works."

"You think, but we don't know."

Chow and Holzgraf exchanged looks of consternation.

"We have to assume the worst. They're trying to figure out a way to neutralize the beam," insisted Chow.

"Figure out the way our signals interact, our moiré pattern," added Holzgraf.

Secretary Rutledge was curious. "And what if they do, what does that mean?"

Garibaldi waved his hands around. "They might be able to render our only weapon ineffective."

Marianne Sarzeau slept late, and then spent a while at breakfast with her family. She arrived in the command post while the debate was just getting hot.

"Look, people. Worried?" she inquired. "We should be. The other side staged an attack. Looks like they had a purpose, knew what they were doing. I don't like it. We need to test our defense."

Barney Wyatt was philosophical. "I don't see a problem. We've still got our heavy artillery. Blow those bots away if we decide to do it."

Rutledge was alarmed by the idea. "No, no. We certainly don't want to resort to gunfire."

Congreve joined the group, having just come from a field hospital set up behind the helipad. He was in a grim mood. "Captain Donaldson will live," he announced, to much relief. "But tendons were torn in his right arm. He's lost a lot of blood. He's in pain."

Upshaw noted the simmering anger. "What do you want to do, Russ? We're of two different minds here."

Congreve spread his arms out. "Let's see how the day goes. I'm not ready to start a fight. But I wouldn't mind showing these arrogant bastards who rightfully rules the world."

▼

Later in the day, the figure who was once Lockwood made another appearance. He didn't announce himself, but stood on the wrecked car again, surveying the human presence, its guns, its vehicles, structures, personnel. After a couple of minutes people took notice. The soldiers on patrol gathered nearby, wave guns and assault rifles at the ready.

Once he had some attention, Lockwood raised his arms in greeting. His amplified voice echoed around the area.

"Good day to our hosts," said he, without a hint of irony.

Holly Chow was out the door of the command post and off to the perimeter fence as soon as she saw the figure.

"Hey, there — that you, Jim? It's me, Holly, remember?"

Lockwood stared at her for a while without any expression. Then he continued with his pre-planned speech.

"Good day, I say again. I see military ordnance, serious weapons, trained on us. As you must have noticed, we have weapons as well. Let's not use them. Instead, we should get to know each other better."

Chow waved her hand around. "Come on, Jim, what are you doing over there? Your old friends at ITF want an explanation."

Lockwood stared at her again. He might have been trying to recall an elusive memory, but neither Chow nor her colleagues in the command post could tell for sure.

"That thing," grumbled Garibaldi, "looks like Jim, got our lingo. But, no. A wolf in sheep's clothing."

"Literally!" said Holzgraf. "And we're just a flock of human sheep."

Congreve's hands tightened into fists at his side.

"You, Holzgraf. Got your waver?"

"Right here, sir."

"All right. Put on a vest and get out there, look protective near Holly, and give that bad boy a blast. Let's see what happens."

Rutledge sputtered objections, which Congreve dismissed with an outstretched palm.

"Take it easy, Mr. Secretary. This guy has been dissolved twice already, so we won't be doing any real harm. I want to know if we still have the capability. We might need it."

Holzgraf joined his fiancée at the perimeter. Half concealed behind her back, he raised his wave gun and sprayed a burst of microwaves at Lockwood.

The alien ambassador wavered, then recovered. He laughed mechanically.

"I felt that," he said. "But the weapon you're using is obsolete. I believe that's the term — obsolete. Yes. Now that you know, let's proceed in a more civilized manner, shall we?"

He looked out over the armed soldiers, past Chow and Holzgraf, and pointed to the command post.

"I know important officials are here today. And many people whose job it is to spread the news of our arrival. Come forward if you will. I'd like to describe our presence here and some of the reasons for it."

Sarzeau, Upshaw, Melrose, and Garibaldi, all of them looking bulky and uncomfortable in the flak jackets General Congreve made them wear, descended from the command post and filed up to the perimeter fence.

As they approached, what appeared to be three men and a woman came out of the Quonset hut and stood near Lockwood.

They might have been former employees of the wrecking yard. Two of them had been dissolved during the night by Captain Donaldson and were now reconstituted by means of mysterious alien technology. Their clothing was ragged and filthy.

Nikki Traeger rushed to join the group. She squeezed through the human delegation and held up a microphone.

"Who are these people?" she demanded. "Why have you kidnapped them?"

Lockwood held out his hands to resist the accusation. "These are colleagues, members of our group, here to maintain our facilities. Work is involved, as it must be for any purpose, on any planet."

Traeger stared at the workers. They stared back. Their faces were devoid of expression.

"You didn't just kidnap them — you murdered them!" she shouted.

Lockwood ignored the charge. "Please, people . . . I'd like you to welcome the Director, who will discuss the matter."

Glittery Brom-Kat-Su glided forth on his hoverboard and stationed himself at Lockwood's side.

"You are correct, woman of the news," intoned the robot. "The biological entities are gone. But the workers you see here, who have joined our cause — in all their former capacity and individuality, they are still alive."

Gasps erupted from the assembled humans over this outrageous claim.

Brom was unmoved. "And more — they are now immortal. Please don't attempt to ruin their transformation. It is our gift."

Murmurs of horror and sardonic laughter rose in the air as the crowd edged backward and away from the illustrious Director and his cold pronouncements.

"What are a few casualties," wondered Brom rhetorically,

"when the sacrifice has produced this happy meeting? Two strains of beings, born from the same mother."

Traeger advanced until she was pressing against the chain link fence separating humans from aliens. She aimed a smartphone camera at the visitors and began recording video.

"Your spokesman here, master of ceremonies seems like, he said you would explain. You speak our language very well . . . so let's hear it."

But, at a signal from Lockwood, Brom turned around and returned to the Quonset hut without another word.

In the command post, Barney Wyatt shook his head. "That robot, what a diplomat."

"Yes," agreed Rutledge. "Not one for tact. The actual humans are dead, but look . . . those folks, they're moving around. For all we know, they have in fact achieved some kind of immortality."

Congreve pulled a microphone on a long boom up close to his lips, which were quivering. "You, Lockwood, your companions, your masters, whoever they are, now hear this — I am hereby imposing a strict quarantine on your outpost. Be advised — nothing and no one shall be on our side of the wire after nightfall. Any violators will suffer the consequences."

Lockwood waved toward the command post to show he heard the general's announcement over the army's very loud public address system.

"Our Director is not a political figure," returned Lockwood in his own artificially enhanced voice, "and he is not familiar with the proper way to express himself. He will learn. Meanwhile, as a gesture of goodwill we're prepared to offer a tour of our base, show we're benign. Select a delegation — we can accept up to six observers."

17

SO, IT'S their *base* now," grumbled Congreve disdainfully. "You heard that? They're staking a claim. What happened to our wrecking yard? Yes, and the sovereign authority of the U.S.A.?"

General Congreve had convened his NITCOM officers, advisors, and government overseers in an auxiliary trailer a quarter mile back from the perimeter to prevent hostilities, should they erupt unexpectedly, from wiping out his brain trust. They were there to decide the question of a tour, and Congreve was not convinced that the offer was made in good faith.

National Security Advisor Melrose stood up to speak.

"With your permission, General."

He stuck his hands in his pockets.

"Allow me to summarize our position. We have a number of experts at our disposal — military, technical, scientific, documentary and, if I am properly informed, even supernatural. That gives us multiple ways to evaluate our situation, but it also means that we are a diverse group of humans, prone to argument and waffling.

"The President is well aware of our competing interests, and he has authorized me to convey his good wishes as Commander-in-Chief in the form of orders. As long as conditions are volatile, turbulent, uncertain — pick your own adjective — everyone involved reports to General Congreve. We're all part of NITCOM now, and military discipline will be enforced."

Gripes and grumbles filled the air.

"I know, I know. Can't be helped. To start our discussion, let's go around the room. Who's in favor of a tour?"

He pointed to Chow. "You first, young lady."

Chow bit her lip. "Looks dangerous. Maybe it's a trap. The idea scares me. Not in favor."

Holzgraf was next. "What Holly said, except — we gotta do it."
Chow punched him on the arm. He gave her a kiss.

Garibaldi was in favor. Weatherall, Upshaw, and Wyatt as well.

Secretary Rutledge shook his head to vote no.

"General Congreve?"

Congreve was busy decoding the national security advisor's little speech. The implied vote of confidence sounded suspicious, and he concluded that the President was singling him out to take the fall in case the NITCOM operation became embarrassing. "I'll vote with the majority," he said.

"And General Weaver?"

Weaver shrugged. "I'm not the one to ask. It's up to Marianne, what she thinks is best . . ."

Melrose lifted his eyebrows in her direction.

"I don't sense trouble, no obvious subterfuge," said Sarzeau. "They're worried we'll just blow them away. They're courting us, currying favor. I would be too if I were them. Let's go, see what we can see."

Melrose crossed his arms. "Seven to two. Call me number eight. This is a golden opportunity to gather intelligence. But it's a risk. Big one. So, who goes?"

After some further discussion, Garibaldi, Holzgraf, Weatherall, and Wyatt were selected.

Secretary Rutledge finished a quiet call on his mobile phone. He raised his hand. "Changed my mind, Walter. I understand the Australian prime minister will be arriving shortly. The Russian ambassador as well. We need to establish our priority here on American soil."

Congreve shook his head. "No senior people, Mr. Secretary. Someone like you gets detained or killed, that's how wars start."

Rutledge was adamant. "Maybe the bots know that, and maybe

they don't want a fight. Maybe my presence will guarantee our delegation's safety."

Melrose rolled his eyes. "What about it, General?"

Congreve sucked on his teeth. "Okay, but should we lose our most senior government official, that's the trigger we pull to wipe these things from the face of the Earth."

NITCOM's military minds loathed the press whenever it got in their hair and expressed their distaste with pungent epithets. But there was general agreement that the historic tour demanded media participation — "for fucking posterity."

Congreve scowled. "Who's running the fourth estate around here?"

Moments later Bob Harrigan, the national anchor for ABC News, was ushered into the trailer. Who did he think might best fill the reportorial bill?

"Well, hell, there's only one choice. That local woman from KTVK, right here in Phoenix. She's whip-smart, doesn't know quit, broke the story in the first place. What's her name? I met her just the other day. Ahh, wait, wait . . . Nico-something . . . Nicolette Traeger."

▼

When the Australian prime minister discovered that Secretary of State Rutledge was on the tour, he regretfully yielded his request to join the human delegation. Secretly, he was much relieved to dodge the politically rewarding but dangerous assignment. Russian Ambassador Fyodor Gavrilov, on the other hand, insisted. In the generous spirit of human unity, he bumped Holzgraf and became the sixth and final member of the troupe.

It took the better part of a week to prepare for the big tour. Anticipation built day by day, fueled in large measure by Traeger's evening TV reports.

"You know what we need?" queried Traeger, sitting in the middle of a newsroom conference with Julia Maxwell and a dozen other major media representatives.

"What's that, my dear?" wondered Bob Harrigan between bites of pizza. He was on his third slice. The theoretically historic moments of the past month were already digested. His question was an idle one, but of some import to journalists in need of talking points and verbal shorthand to make sense of the tremendous events they were describing every day, all day long.

"We need a name. Name for these aliens, extraterrestrials, visitors, whatever."

Harrigan swallowed the last of his pizza. He took a sip of lemonade. "Okay, a name. Good idea." His eyes seemed to lose focus. He twisted his lips into a knot. Then, "Interstellar robots, from another star. How about, *starbot,* or *starbots* as the case may be?"

"Wow," said Maxwell.

"I like it! Starbots! Star-fucking-Bots!" declared Traeger. "Very quick, Mr. Bob — now we know why ABC pays you the big bucks."

No one objected, and so, by unspoken journalistic decree, the first aliens to visit Planet Earth became known to one and all as the starbots.

▼

On D-Day, at H-Hour, the human volunteers selected to tour the starbot base strode out from a marshaling trailer in fashionable sky blue jumpsuits, with white baseball caps on their heads, reflective sunglasses over their eyes, and surgical gloves on their hands. HEPA-filtered dust masks hung around their collars, just in case. Rutledge and Wyatt wore first aid kits on little fanny packs. Weatherall was carrying small oxygen tanks in a backpack. Garibaldi gripped his smartphone in one hand, and Traeger had a 50-

megapixel digital camera on a strap around her neck.

High above, their progress was covered by Ted Purley in the KTVK helicopter and annotated by the affable comments of Bob Harrigan. The nation and the world were watching.

What the world did not see was less obvious. Traeger's camera was hopeful gear, but technicians had also fashioned a tiny video camera into a button on the chest pocket of her jump suit. Garibaldi was wearing an audio recorder in his ear instead of a hearing aid he didn't need. Gavrilov was carrying an ID card that was actually a probe designed to attach airborne chemical samples to its glossy surface. Being cautious, NITCOM's leaders expected treachery, and were hoping to outfox the bots.

One by one the group filed through an opening in the perimeter fence of the wrecking yard, where they were met by the transformed figure who was once James Lockwood, and who was now referred to as *Jimbot* or *the Lockbot,* or, more generally, as one of the ersatz humans everyone, following another example of journalistic shorthand, was now calling the *sandos.*

He led the group through a maze of rusting automobile carcasses to the wide entrance of the Stone Valley Scrap & Salvage Quonset hut. Once they were out of sight, no one saw or heard them again for three long hours.

Ted Purley was forced to refuel his helicopter in order to keep a video vigil. In a makeshift studio near the NITCOM command post, Bob Harrigan was running out of anecdotes.

"We were hoping that Doctor Garibaldi would be able to give us progress reports," said Harrigan. "Is cell service dead in there? Steel building, after all, or did the starbots disable or possibly confiscate his phone?"

Harrigan leaned forward in his chair for a close examination of his TV monitor.

"But wait a minute, who do I see coming out of that Quonset

hut? Looks like — most surely is — our intrepid adventurers. I count two, three, five . . . where's Rutledge? But, yes, trailing a step behind, here comes the Secretary of State, just back on Earth after the most important diplomatic foray in human history. There's a wave! Smiles! Baseball caps held high! What a relief for America, for the whole world. We're all taking a deep breath here, everyone back outside, safe and sound."

18

JUST BEFORE the tour group arrived back at the trailer where they started from, Secretary Rutledge called them into a huddle.

"We've seen things, strange and impressive things that no one else has ever seen. Starbot relations are delicate. Let's frame our report in positive terms and avoid anything shocking, anything that might start a war. Understood? Agreed?"

Nods all around. They already knew.

Once they were inside and out of sight of media surveillance, Congreve assembled them for a thorough debriefing.

To start the process Guy Holzgraf powered up a wave gun and painted each member of the tour with a cascade of microwaves. Traeger and Gavrilov protested angrily, but no one dissolved.

"What's the point, General?" griped Wyatt. "You saw how Mr. Sandman weathered the storm. We know our ray gun has been neutralized."

Congreve nodded. "Of course, but we try to be thorough."

Chow activated a video camera to record the session. Upshaw noted the date, time, and names of the participants.

"All right, let's hear it. What's going on in there? What did you see?"

Wyatt looked at his fellow tourists, did not see anyone else volunteering, and cleared his throat.

"There was some kind of security gate. Very weird, because when I stepped through I seemed to be in a long white corridor. Brightly lit. Lenses and funny little antennas or something watched me move along through it."

Congreve raised a hand. "Hold it right there. How about the rest of you? Same experience?"

Nods from all of them.

Traeger took up the thread. "We found out that all of the

starbots are made here. Right here on Earth, in that Quonset hut."

"That's right," added Weatherall. "The blueprints come from their home planet. First, they used those signals my colleagues at Goldstone picked up to make a machine, and that machine made another machine, and that machine made them."

"Makes them," said Garibaldi. "It's still going on."

Traeger shifted around in her chair. "The crazy part is this — get ready — they insist that their biological ancestors paid us a visit a couple of hundred thousand years ago, when their planet still had some air to breathe. They claim those aliens edited our DNA. Improved the species. Why we're not apes anymore."

This statement rocked the stay-at-home contingent. Congreve and Upshaw glanced at each other. Both frowned.

"That's some claim."

"Bullshit, you ask me."

Sarzeau was as stunned and disturbed as the rest of them. "This is ridiculous. They're worried about us, currying favor, like I thought. Buying time. Who knows why."

"What about our spy gear?"

Wyatt waved a dismissive hand. "They took Nikki's camera, took Garibaldi's phone, took our oxygen cylinders, and both our first aid kits."

"I still have ID," said Gavrilov. "Aliens, *zvezdnyy roboty*, not so smart, *da?*"

"The button camera? Voice recorder?"

"I don't think they noticed," said Traeger.

"Then let's have a look."

Chow rolled a beaded screen down from the trailer ceiling.

Holzgraf cut the video button from Traeger's jumpsuit. He inserted it into a receptacle on a video projector, added Garibaldi's phony hearing aid, and threw a switch.

Grainy images of the long corridor moved on the screen,

interrupted now and again by colorful MPEG artifacts.

Then Brom-Kat-Su appeared to welcome his guests. His voice was loud and raspy.

"Here is our receiver."

Brom pointed to a steel-grey boxlike device attached to a tall antenna. Then he turned, pointed to another device.

"Here is our purifier, where dirt becomes minerals we can use."

He turned again and pointed to a third device, larger than the other two, and of a complex shape. Tube-like structures ran here and there over a surface covered with mysterious humps and bumps.

"Here is our main fabricator, where our workers and I were manufactured. Designed from afar, but as you see, made here on Earth."

While the humans watched the shaky video in the comfort and safety of the NITCOM trailer, an object emerged from the fabricator. It was a small headless robot, the size of a suitcase. It rolled away out of sight on a pair of wheels.

"Look at that!" marveled Chow.

"Next time, we could be seeing a cannon pop out," grumped Upshaw, "if they decide to play rough."

"Anyone notice Brom's voice?" asked Melrose. "I hear the same tones coming from your former colleague. Same timbre and speech patterns. No individuality as we understand it."

On the screen, Brom turned away to his alien duties, and the Lockwood sando moved close to Traeger's button camera.

"What my glorious leader didn't say is this — we were all created by the same entities, our precursors."

Garibaldi's hidden microphone picked up Traeger scoffing at the idea. "This is a joke — some kind of biblical joke."

The Lockbot shook his head emphatically.

"No joke, Ms. Traeger . . ."

▼

After Congreve and company were finished quizzing them, the tour group members were dismissed for medical exams, showers, and clean clothes. The stay-at-homes mulled what they had learned. They were in a pensive mood.

"The DNA thing — could it happen?" Upshaw was shaken and disturbed by the idea.

"Sure it could," said Garibaldi, even more disturbed. "Edit our DNA? We're doing some of that ourselves. You've heard of CRISPR, right? It's a hot new field, and sure to get hotter."

"Jesus Christ."

"What about our *touristas?*" growled Melrose. "They were in the devil's den, out of contact, for three hours. We know the starbot capabilities . . ."

He let the thought hang.

"They must be watched," declared Sarzeau, voicing the uneasy concerns of her colleagues.

19

DR. GARIBALDI spent some time in the evenings on patrol with the NITCOM sentries, playing an ultraviolet flashlight over the perimeter of the Stone Valley Scrap & Salvage wrecking yard. He ignored the occasional scorpion glowing in his beam, but whenever he observed a grain of sand glinting on the desert floor he snagged it with a tiny plastic spoon and bagged it in a plastic pouch. Within a few days he had himself a few milligrams of sparkly alien material.

Acting upon inquiries made by Holly Chow, he located an X-ray diffraction machine and an electron microscope on the Arizona State University campus in Tempe. There he subjected his samples to analysis and reported his results to the NITCOM brain trust.

"The sand grains — what are they? How do they work?" As a military man forced into a defensive posture, Congreve was bothered by his ignorance of the starbots' motives and capabilities.

Professorial Garibaldi, on the other hand, was too enthusiastic about his research to be so bothered.

"It's all very clever. Each grain is actually a conglomeration of many smaller grains, easily made from common materials found in our soils. Think of it — made from *dirt*.

"Hidden in their crystalline structure are a number of foreign atoms. Aluminum, cobalt, iodine, magnesium, zinc, for example. Their positions tell the grains how to assemble into the various bots and sandos we see. The information density is comparable to — far exceeds, really — that of DNA."

Congreve clasped his hands and arched his back. "How do we disrupt their activity, now that our wave guns don't work? Tell me that, please."

Garibaldi slumped. "Their weakness is the chemical bonds

between the interior metals. Microwave energy should be sufficient to break them. But, the starbots have somehow hardened our targets, changed the bonding frequencies."

"I'll tell you how we can disrupt the bastards," asserted Holzgraf. "With bombs. Big ones."

Secretary Rutledge turned pale. "No, absolutely not. These so-called starbots could still be our friends."

"Friends? Jesus, Morey," growled Congreve.

But Rutledge was insistent. "Look at it this way — if they are robots, and we think they are — and if their experience tells them that lost souls can be reconstituted at will — something we know they do — then their grasp of biological frailties may be . . . less than perfect. Yes, they have killed a few people. We need to look past that ugly fact."

Upshaw recoiled from the Secretary's argument, was about to protest, then held his tongue.

Chow rolled her eyes. "Let's remember — Jimbot, the Lockbot, whoever Jim Lockwood is now — he doesn't behave or sound like our old pal from days of yore. He's just one of the sandos now — no longer human."

Holzgraf was even grimmer. "Mo mentioned dead bodies down there in Marana, Mr. Secretary — those boys who stole our sandy remains weren't transformed. Not like Lockwood. They were duplicated and killed."

Wyatt rubbed hands together. "When did anyone ever establish a foreign policy for aliens? Until now, the idea was a ridiculous fantasy. I'm here to help insure public safety, and the best way to do that is problematic. Who knows? The Secretary might be onto something. Maybe the starbots won't be our friends. But maybe we can help each other. Figure out a *quid pro quo.*"

"If we had any idea why they decided to pay us a visit," sighed Melrose.

General Weaver turned to Sarzeau, who was hovering in the background, nursing a can of Sprite. "Well — any odd vibe we should know about?"

Sarzeau shook her head. "I feel low-grade tension on both sides. But don't look at me to solve our problems. The feeling is faint, comes from everywhere. It's probably natural."

20

NIKKI TRAEGER was getting ready for a TV show featuring a dozen reporters from a dozen countries who were covering the alien presence. An *ABC Special Presentation* to bring America and the world up to speed was about to go on the air, its purpose being to calm everyone, to neutralize the idea of an *infestation,* or even worse, an *invasion.*

After makeup was applied and hair blown into shape, but before the cameras rolled, Traeger sat down beside Bob Harrigan for a preliminary conference.

"Listen, Bob, I'm going to make an announcement during the show."

Harrigan, the appointed moderator, was instantly on his guard. "An announcement . . ."

"Yup. Betraying my loyalty to NITCOM, I guess, and upholding my duty to the media, to the people, to truth."

"What in the world?"

"You'll hear it. You might not like it, might hate me for it. Can me afterward, if that's your pleasure. Just don't kill my mike while I'm talking. Deal?"

Harrigan frowned. After a slow think, the frown turned into a sly grin. "You've got something, you chirpy bird. While you were in the lion's den. Hah! What is it? I can't wait to hear." He slapped the table top. "This show is going to out-rate the Super Bowl."

Traeger patted him on the shoulder and slumped into her chair.

The show's assistant director, standing behind the studio camera, held up his hand, counting down with his fingers: three, two, one, go!

Harrigan leaned forward and posed for the camera.

"Good evening, ladies and gentlemen, my fellow Americans, citizens of the world. Tonight we have the privilege of chatting with a group of dedicated newshounds who have spent every waking moment for a month covering the most amazing single event in human history. The starbots are here! How about that, huh? Does that make your tummy tingle? Keep you awake at night? I know it does me. Superstition is natural, but not that helpful. Let's hear some candid impressions from the frontline observers, conquer our fears with some facts . . ."

Harrigan started the session off by calling upon Gwendolyn Nash, a BBC correspondent, who dispassionately reviewed what everyone already knew in crisp round tones. Her presentation was greeted by perfunctory applause from the studio audience.

Toshiyasu Ogawa, a handsome young Japanese reporter for NHK, was next. He expressed his nation's doubts and worries in an incomprehensible accent, focusing grimly on the dangers of an alien manufacturing plant operating without human oversight.

Harrigan knew that TV, even documentary TV, was nothing if not showbiz, and he was eager to find a competent English speaker for his largely English-speaking audience.

"No oversight," he repeated. "That's a concern, no doubt. Is the concern justified? Let's hear now from someone who has firsthand knowledge, one of the heroic few who dared to venture inside the alien operation, see for herself what's going on in there . . . KTVK's famous news anchor, Nicolette Traeger."

Traeger acknowledged a burst of hearty applause with a wave.

"Hello, everyone. Yes, with my friends on the tour, I saw the starbot fabricator. We all saw the thing. It works, and we don't have anything like it. Who knows how our encounter will play out? Maybe they'll help us build one."

She glanced nervously at Harrigan, gave him a little nod — here I go, off the deep end.

"But that's not what I want to talk about. We saw their machinery, very impressive, and we also heard a tale that, if true, is much more important. As we all know by now, the starbots are mechanical creatures. And they have their version of a biblical story, how they were created by creatures made out of flesh and blood, like us."

Oohs and ahhs from the studio audience.

"That's not all. They insist that we are related, distant cousins if you will."

Murmurs of disapproval floated around the room.

"Sounds impossible, right? Sounds like self-serving propaganda. But they aren't trying out some political metaphor. I doubt they know what a metaphor is. Instead, they make a claim — a big one — that modern humans arose when the starbot creators visited Planet Earth some two hundred thousand years ago." Traeger paused, took a deep breath. "When they edited and improved the DNA that makes us who we are today."

Roars of shock and disbelief echoed through the studio. Bob Harrigan's face turned pale. "Well now, Ms. Traeger, that's quite a tale. Perhaps we ought to leave it —"

Traeger shot out an arm and upraised hand to forestall the interruption.

"— Hear me out, please. I am as skeptical as everyone in this room. But there's more. Looks like those ancient creators shared at least one trait with us human beings — vanity. According to the starbots, they left a *signature* in our DNA. Signed their handiwork."

Groans and angry shouts filled the air.

"A signature?" scoffed Harrigan. "Really . . ."

"I know. Absurd. But they were specific. We were told to take a close look at chromosome five."

"Chromosome five! God in Heaven!" sputtered Harrigan.

Traeger spread her hands. "I hope some ambitious microbiologist will do just that. Back me up or prove me wrong."

21

LOCK THE BITCH UP!" fumed Congreve. "Make her swallow the damn key. Or send her to Moscow, see how she likes living next to that fuck Snowden."

"Take it easy, Russ," cautioned Upshaw. "She crossed the line, but . . ."

"But nothing!" The NITCOM commander was beside himself. "This is betrayal. Fucking reporters!"

National Security Advisor Melrose was coldly furious. "I had already contracted with our lab in Bethesda to check out this DNA idea, give us a chance to rebut the starbot claim with solid evidence. And Nancy has quietly arranged a backup through friends at Stanford. Now this."

"Let's hope one of them comes through," said Weatherall. "This is going to turn into an unseemly race."

Secretary of State Rutledge was amused by his colleagues' negative reactions. "Bravo, I say. Well, maybe not right out loud to the President when I brief him, but here among friends, oh yes, yes indeed."

"Are you nuts?"

"That woman Traeger? She has done us a service. People want to know the truth, even if it hurts. Now they'll have it, one way or the other."

"This is a circus. People will feel a psychological blow. We'll see suicides, riots. Calls to annihilate the starbots, for sure."

Rutledge sighed. "Oh, I doubt that. Truth has a calming effect, you'll see."

Within a week, the race was over. Medical Instructor Vijay Sunipam, a post-doc lecturer at Duke University, called a press conference to announce an important discovery.

"Using our lab's new sequencer, plus computer software I wrote that scans through the human genome at unprecedented speed, my Duke colleagues and I have identified a stretch of DNA in human chromosome five that consists exclusively of thymine-adenine base pairs."

He stepped through a series of colorful PowerPoint slides showing DNA nucleotides and their hydrogen bond pairings.

"This sequence, far from the nearest gene-encoding region, is seventy-seven base pairs long and is isolated by the normal genetic stop signals."

A reporter for *Cell*, the prestigious peer-reviewed journal for biological discoveries, raised a hand.

"Yes?"

"It's not that unusual to find genetic sequences with just two base pairs. Please explain."

"No, you're right. But this sequence on chrome-five is unique. Nothing else like it anywhere. At first we thought we might be looking at a coded signature. Dots and dashes stuff. But we weren't getting anywhere. Then it occurred to me that the signers might know how hard it is to decode an actual name. So, I thought — how about a picture? I decided to turn the one-dimensional string into a two-dimensional grid. And what do you know? We have a result . . ."

The *Cell* reporter didn't believe a word.

"A picture? That sounds like one of those *ancient astronaut* conspiracy theories. How do you know? We want proof."

The junior researcher wasn't fazed. He shrugged. "Here's a clue for you. Seventy-seven has just two factors, seven and eleven."

"So . . ?"

"So — a grid of seventy-seven dots can only be seven-by-eleven or eleven-by-seven. Those are the only arrangements that work. Any other pattern has dots left over. I brought a slide . . ."

With the airy self-confidence of youth, the Duke researcher blithely pressed a button on his laptop and advanced his Power-Point presentation to a diagrammatic image:

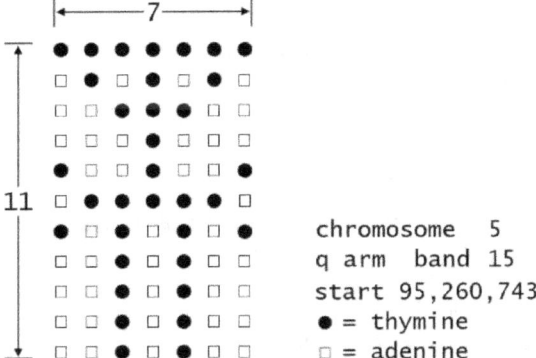

Gasps issued from the astonished reporters. Nevertheless, once they recovered their composure, the veteran science writers remained skeptical. They brought up all sorts of cynical objections, including the ugly possibility of fraud. Converting them into believers required another week and corroborating results from half a dozen other labs.

Not all the sequences were perfect, as geneticists from Harvard, Cal, USC, Oxford, the Sorbonne, Tsinghua University, and others discovered when they took up the challenge. Their efforts led to some intriguing discoveries. Many Asian people, for example, showed a blank in position seventy-six. Native Americans and Baltic Europeans sometimes recorded cytosine-guanine base pairs in positions thirty-seven and forty-nine, leading to speculation about an unsuspected close relationship. Africans occasionally lost an entire row of nucleotides, scrambling the alien legs.

Soon, the Duke diagram became the most-reproduced picture in a hundred years, inspiring TV show concepts and big-budget movie plans. Before a month was out, it was the most widely disseminated news release in history.

People everywhere, humbled by the genetic revelation, frightened by its implications, and yet smugly aware of their starry heritage, were in a state of awe unknown since the middle ages.

▼

Malcolm Dutton, the Australian prime minister, was preparing to return to his duties down under when a reporter for the *Arizona Republic* cornered him in the first class lounge at Sky Harbor International Airport in Phoenix.

"You came all the way from Australia to visit the starbot site, is that right?"

"Yes, a pilgrimage."

Do you wish you had taken the tour, sir?"

"Well, I envy those who did. Maybe our visitors will organize another one."

"Are you worried about them, what they might do?"

Dutton smiled.

"Not at all. I see no evidence of hostility."

"What about the fatalities?"

"We have seen a few. Misunderstanding. Regrettable."

"Think we'll nuke 'em?"

"I hope not. Nuking? War? Isn't that the main curse of the human race? I look upon this, the biggest event in history, as a page-turner. But threat? Nightmare scenario, possible takeover . . . I think we're a threat to ourselves. And takeover? Let it happen! We could use a Leviathan to get us out of our Hobbesian trap, force us to become civilized, take our place as citizens of the galaxy."

The reporter was surprised by the prime minister's candid remarks.

"Whoa, isn't that being naïve?"

"I don't think so. It's a historic opportunity."

Phase **3**

22

ZERO HOUR at Stone Valley Scrap & Salvage.

Flood lights illuminating the vast expanse of wrecked vehicles.

Soldiers on patrol.

No incidents to report.

At two hundred hours, however, a large section of the Quonset hut roof slowly and silently opened.

In a trailer almost half a mile away, the sleepy army specialist on duty rubbed his eyes and toggled a control to zoom in on the event through three different surveillance cameras.

Some sort of antenna poked upward through the opening. It turned slowly around once and then withdrew. The specialist picked up his phone.

"General? Sorry to wake you."

He paused while a groggy General Congreve collected his wits.

"Christ, son, I'm asleep. Call my aide . . ."

"Protocol, sir. You established it. We have activity, purpose unknown, on top of the Quonset hut."

"What? You recording this?"

"Yes, sir, three cameras. Might want to take a look, sir."

Five minutes later Congreve, Upshaw, Weaver, and Wyatt were assembled in the NITCOM command post, drinking strong coffee while they watched the Quonset hut through binoculars.

The reported hole in the roof wasn't visible from their position. But every few minutes a bat flew over the area and was briefly lit up by a shaft of light from inside the building, confirming the existence of an opening. Otherwise, nothing. The surveillance warning seemed like a false alarm.

Suddenly a large shape flew out of the Quonset hut and disappeared into the night sky, its rapid passage made indistinct by motion blur.

"What the fuck was that?" blurted Wyatt.

"Some kind of vehicle. Ship? Drone?"

"Awfully big. Jesus."

"I didn't see any wings."

Walter Melrose was late to the vigil. By the time he arrived, the excitement was over, and all was calm again.

"What is it? What did I miss?"

Upshaw shook his head. "Something flew out of a hole on top of the Quonset hut over there. High speed. We barely got a glimpse."

The group hiked to the surveillance trailer and reviewed the event several times on several cameras. Even when played in slow motion, details were invisible. A very large object of some kind certainly flew up and out of the Quonset hut. But its nature and purpose were obscured by its startling velocity.

"That thing big enough to carry a starbot, you think?"

"Definitely," said the specialist operating the cameras. "It's not so blurry we can't get a size. Hull length ten meters, I'd say."

"So much for our video technology."

"Call NORAD. They must have a track."

The officer on duty at the North American Aerospace Defense Command, tucked under protective Cheyenne Mountain in Colorado, checked all five computer screens arrayed around his desk.

"We watched it for about twenty minutes," he reported. "Last position over the Atlantic. Already a hundred kliks up, not too far from Bermuda. Eastbound. Vanished at that point. We've looked at all our satellites, all our radar data. No joy since launch-plus-twenty."

▼

Three days went by without a sighting or any information on the starbot vehicle's trajectory, its destination, or its present whereabouts.

The NITCOM brain trust was beyond frustrated.

"NORAD saw our bogey traverse twenty-five hundred miles in twenty minutes. That's seventy-five hundred miles an hour," noted Garibaldi.

'Your point?" asked Melrose, who struggled with even the simplest technical questions.

"It was moving fast, but it's not in orbit. A satellite launch would be moving its payload more than twice that fast by the time it passed Bermuda."

"Hmm."

Upshaw ventured to the wrecking yard perimeter, raised a bullhorn, and appealed directly and loudly to the alien version of his former assistant James Lockwood. But the alien spokesman did not answer his call. Starbot activity, always secretive except for routine maintenance performed by the sando workers, ceased entirely.

"Where the hell did that thing go?" grumbled Congreve. "Those bumblers at NORAD . . . imagine if Russian missiles were on the way."

"The starbot ship is going to land somewhere. Probably has landed," asserted Garibaldi stoutly. "We're bound to find it, and anyone on board — eventually." He waggled a finger and touched his forehead. "And when we do, we'll find out why they're here."

23

NIGHT in high country.

A waxing Moon rose between scraggly trees, throwing black shadows off rocky outcrops surrounding a grassy valley.

An hour later, a wingless aircraft dropped silently out of a starry sky and landed gently near a stone wall shielding the ruins of an ancient city. A cloud of dust ballooned up.

Gradually the dust cleared, and the object's metallic surface became visible, glimmering in pale moonlight.

A laser beam shot out from one end of the thing. It swept back and forth over the stone wall and the ground around it.

Then, as effortlessly as a big animal standing up from a nap, the vehicle sprouted a set of tank treads, raising more dust. A moment later it rumbled forward, knocking an enormous hole in the wall. Stones crashed down, bouncing off the intruder without creating a single dent.

Guided by laser beam, the vehicle trundled into a field enclosed within the now ruined wall and halted beside a tall conical tower fashioned from dry stone masonry. The treads disappeared into the vehicle's hull. An arm like a backhoe materialized. The vehicle was now an earthmoving machine. It began to dig.

The arm deposited each scoop of earth into an opening in the machine's upper surface. After a few scoops, the machine started to vibrate. Then, in a swift transformation, it doubled in size. A bigger backhoe dug out bigger chunks of dirt, deposited them in a bigger opening, and the entire machine doubled in size again.

▼

A uniformed park ranger out on patrol was drawn to the sound of falling rocks. He made his way to the stone enclosure, discovered the gaping breach in the wall, and cautiously approached the now very large machine and the very large pit that it had created.

He was outraged by the gross vandalism. The area was, after all, a national park, and a World Heritage Site at that.

The ranger had never seen any actual earthmoving equipment in his life, and certainly nothing like the gleaming excavator he now confronted, but he sensed, dimly, that it was otherworldly. He bravely readied his smartphone and photographed the intrusion and the incredible destruction from several points of view. He was sweating with fear.

Once he had good photographic documentation, he tried to call park headquarters and report the situation. But the local phone system was out of order.

Just then the Moon sank behind a high ridge. Long poles bristled suddenly from the machine, and powerful work lights flowered on their ends, casting the area in an orange glow. The digging arm gathered in another bucketful of dirt. The ranger, discombobulated by the strange activity, staggered back. He wiped his brow, took a hesitant step to regain his position, then thought better of the idea and retreated behind the ruins of an ancient stone dwelling.

Sensing movement, the machine's work lights swiveled away from the dig site and fastened on the ranger. Then they went out. A blue laser beam issued forth, speared the man, and quickly scanned his very dark face. He stood without moving, possibly hypnotized.

▼

When the starbot machine started digging, park lights dimmed, then failed. Communications were disrupted. As a result, the ranger's comrades were slow to rouse themselves and organize a search party. When they finally arrived at the dig site, they found their colleague in a catatonic state, standing upright, as stiff and unresponsive as a statue. Valiant attempts to rouse him went unrewarded.

Then they noticed, with a mixture of outrage and fear, the astonishing damage to their park's major artifact. As they moved toward the newly excavated pit, a blue laser transfixed them in its beam, halting them in their tracks.

24

AFTER ONLY a day and a night, the digging machine ceased its efforts, and a troupe of park rangers — or their duplicates — swarmed into the hole it had dug where, using tools spawned from the glittering machine, they removed all remaining dirt, roots, and rock debris.

The cleaned-up dig revealed geometrically perfect stone walls covered with a kind of smooth plaster incised here and there with peculiar symbols. Doorways led away from the pit into rooms that remained underneath the protective cover of undisturbed earth.

Once their labors were finished, the park rangers stood stiffly in a rank while a pair of many-legged robots budded off from the digging machine and crawled down to explore the excavation's depths.

One of the bots discovered a rectangular structure standing in the middle of the furthest back room. It scraped at the edges, found a seam, and pried the cover off what appeared to be a stone sarcophagus.

Its companion then bloomed a projector of some kind on its forward right leg, aimed it at the dried-up corpse within the box, and bathed the thing in blue laser light. The corpse began to writhe and thrash its arms about. The wrinkles faded, and it seemed to come to life. It sat up in its coffin. A triangular head turned toward the robot pair. An arm reached out to them.

Then, as rapidly as it revived, the thing shriveled up and fell back into its resting place.

The two bots became inert. They might have been silently considering the unfortunate result of their actions. Then, after a reflective moment, they both began vibrating uncontrollably, throwing off showers of multicolored particles. Within a few seconds they were reduced to piles of sand.

Outside, the alien machine retracted its digging arm and its stalk-like work lights. It pivoted upward on one end. A pulsing glow suffused the hull. Suddenly, without a sound, it lifted from the grassy field and vaulted into the sky.

▼

In Phoenix, in the offices of KTVK, Nikki Traeger and Julia Maxwell had gotten wind of the starbot ship and NORAD's failure to track it. They were on the phone day and night, calling reporters Traeger had met while on her exotic adventures in Europe, Asia, and the Middle East.

"Hey, Nikk, this guy in Beirut, Independent TV News, Ian Gilmore, says he knows you."

"Ian who?"

"Gilmore."

"Oh yeah, him."

"How well do you know him?"

"I met him once, in a bar in Tel Aviv."

"Ahh . . ." Maxwell looked hurt.

"I don't sleep with everyone, Julie. And never anyone named *Ian.*"

"Well, I think he might be inflating his resumé, if nothing else. Anyway, he wants to talk to you, pass on a tip. We're Skyping, but no video, the connection sucks. Be nice."

Maxwell handed Traeger a telephone headset. Traeger clamped it over her ears.

"Ian! How *are* you?" she purred.

Pause.

"South African. Never met him. Or, whoops, her."

Pause.

"You're fucking kidding me."

Pause.

"You're sure? She's reliable?"

Pause.

"All right, all right. I owe you one, owe you big time. What do you need from me?"

Pause.

"I think Secretary Rutledge is prepping a trip to Ramallah, trying to save a peace deal with the Israelis that will never work. We're pals now, comrades in arms, veterans of the famous Tour. I'll recommend you for a one-on-one, how's that?"

Pause.

"My pleasure. Meantime, dodge those *katyushas,* okay?"

Traeger removed the headset and stared at the wall.

"That was . . . interesting," she said.

Out west of Phoenix, at Stone Valley Scrap & Salvage, General Congreve, General Upshaw, Walter Melrose, and Barney Wyatt were in the NITCOM command post, fretting over their ignorance. In the days since the starbot ship launched, they had learned nothing of its whereabouts.

A polite knock interrupted their harsh assessment of the high-tech fools at NORAD.

Upshaw opened the door.

"Sir? Got someone here claims to have important information."

Upshaw peeked around the door frame. There, standing passively in the strong grip of her military escort, was Nicolette Traeger, the treacherous reporter.

"Well now, look who's here. Got some information? Got some nerve, anyway."

Traeger raised her eyebrows and squinched her lips. "Can I get a hearing?"

Upshaw stretched out an ironic arm to welcome her into the trailer, where the rest of the group gathered to confront her.

Congreve grimaced, unable to conceal his distaste. "I'm willing to listen, but your news better be good."

Traeger folded her arms, not at all intimidated by the cool hostility. "I know where the starbots landed."

"Tell that to NORAD," growled Wyatt.

"It's true. I know, and you don't. But — wild guess — you'd like to know, am I right?"

Congreve set his teeth on edge.

"We'd like to know."

Traeger looked around, spotted an unoccupied swivel chair, and sat herself down.

"Here's the deal. I give you the hotspot, and you agree to embed me with whatever team you're going to deploy there."

Melrose was offended. "You can't expect the armed forces to make a promise like that. It's impossible."

"I don't need a *promise,* gentlemen. I just need to know it will happen."

Congreve took a turn around the tiny room.

"I know you think I blew a secret," she continued, "but I doubled your exposure and inspired the American people to your cause. You should be grateful."

"We should be grateful!" jeered Wyatt. "Will you listen to the woman!"

Congreve stopped in front of Traeger, clasped hands behind his back. He willed himself to swallow his animosity toward the impudent woman without gagging.

"All right, Miss Traeger . . ."

". . . Nikki."

All right, Nikki" — deep breath — "you're in. Maybe not on the first flight, but we'll make several. You'll get there."

Traeger was about to push her luck, then decided to accept the compromise.

"Fair enough. Here's the telegram — the starbots landed in Great Zimbabwe National Park in Zimbabwe, Southern Africa. They've been tearing up the place. Ruins of an ancient city. Big archeological dig. Possible casualties."

"Well . . . I'll be damned."

25

A THREESOME of C-130J Super Hercules cargo airplanes from the 39th Airlift Squadron at Dyess Air Force Base in Abilene, Texas, arrived at Luke Air Force Base on the western outskirts of Phoenix after a two-hour flight.

There, not all that far from the Stone Valley Scrap & Salvage site, NITCOM loaded up vehicles, weapons, and personnel for the trip to Zimbabwe.

It was a long trip, and a complex undertaking. The fleet accomplished the mission in forty hours, twenty-seven in the air flying at four hundred miles an hour, with six stops to refuel, and with permissions hastily gathered to cross the airspace of a dozen countries.

Secretary of State Rutledge was forced to use all his diplomatic skills to extract a reluctant (but ultimately grateful) invitation from the government of Zimbabwe to land a small force and investigate the unprecedented activities in Great Zimbabwe National Park, the cultural crown jewel of the nation.

General Upshaw, the officer in charge of the expedition, had plenty of time on the long flight to brief himself on the mission target.

Great Zimbabwe, he learned, consisted of the ruined walls of numerous stone buildings stretching over a couple thousand acres. The centerpiece of the park was the Great Enclosure, where a nearly circular stone wall eighty meters in diameter surrounded the elaborate ruins of several buildings and a mysterious conical monument that towered ten meters above the ground.

The builders, expert stone masons, were probably ancestors of the Shona people, and the structure may have once been the seat of kings, but its actual provenance was lost to history, and so, being majestic and crumbling into ruin at the same time, it seemed incredibly ancient. In fact it was only a thousand years old. Even so, it was the oldest, largest, and most refined architectural achievement in all of sub-Sahara Africa before the modern era . . . hence its status as a national treasure. Why the builders chose its obscure location was a matter of debate.

▼

The airplanes all made *maximum effort landings* on the very short runway at the Masvingo regional airport, and the NITCOM detachment motored thirty kilometers from there to the historical park in a convoy of armored personnel carriers.

What they found upon their arrival was a small hybrid force composed of men from the Zimbabwe Republic Police, the ZRP, and a squad of lightly armored vehicles from the Zimbabwe National Army, the ZNA. They were standing guard at the park entrance.

General Upshaw stepped out of a jeep all decked out in his rarely worn Air Force uniform. He approached what he hoped was the senior Zimbabwe commander, a short round man in a lavishly decorated uniform topped by an orange beret.

"Hello, I'm Upshaw. This is my team." He waved at the American convoy, then held out his hand. The officer took it and gave it a heartfelt shake.

"Colonel Felix Mobanda. Welcome to Zimbabwe, General."

Upshaw noticed that the entrance to the park was barred.

"Who's in there?" he inquired.

"No one, sir. What you are calling the 'starbots,' they have departed, but my men are not willing to enter the park premises."

"Still some of the opposition around, you think?"

"We don't know. We hope not."

Upshaw was relieved and also disappointed. NITCOM was late to the party.

"How long since the bots took off, got a time hack?"

Mobanda looked at his watch. "Thirty-six hours, maybe. Before our team arrived. Radar in Harare saw a blip, but it disappeared before we could compute a flight path. We have anxiously been awaiting your arrival."

"All right, then. Per agreement negotiated by Secretary Rutledge, we are prepared to enter the park and investigate. It will look better to all concerned, your government and mine, if you and your men join us."

Mobanda swallowed hard. "Many of my men believe ghosts still haunt the ancient city and, now awakened, will take vengeance upon trespassers."

"I don't believe in ghosts, Colonel." declared Upshaw, who then remembered his experiences with Marianne Sarzeau. "Well, no hauntings, anyway."

Mobanda nodded. "Be assured, we will overcome our fears."

With the formal exchange of credentials out of the way, Upshaw led the combined teams to the base of the masonry tower, which he recognized from his briefing materials, and peered down into the depths of the starbot dig. He gave out a long low whistle of amazement.

Dr. Weatherall, the only member of Upshaw's ITF group on the expedition, was equally stunned.

"This is extraordinary. How long were the starbots here? They dug this hole in less than a week!"

Milling about on the floor of the dig were a dozen park rangers, the same ones who tidied up the dig for the alien visitors.

Upshaw readied one of the team's wave guns, and pointed it into the pit,

"Just to be sure, you know . . ."

He pressed the trigger. A high-pitched whine issued from the weapon, and an invisible cone of microwaves washed over the park rangers.

"Hah! No effect," groaned Weatherall.

"They're just people," argued Upshaw.

Weatherall suspected otherwise. "They don't behave like people. I think they're sandos."

"What are you talking about?" queried Mobanda, moving up beside the Americans. He eyed their strange weapon with great curiosity.

"This thing, it will kill the starbots?"

Weatherall shook her head. "That was the theory, but the bots have figured out a countermeasure."

"And you think my compatriots, these rangers, they are infected in some way?"

"We'll never know, I'm afraid," said Upshaw sadly.

"How could that be? These are my people!" insisted Mobanda, rejecting the possibility.

One of the rangers began to climb out of the dig site on a narrow ladder. It swayed and flexed under his weight, drawing the onlookers' scrutiny and causing them to hold their breath. Then, a few rungs from the top, the ranger collapsed into a shower of sand that fell away, bouncing off the wall, raining down on his fellows below.

"Oh my Good God Lord Jesus in Heaven!" exclaimed Mobanda, crossing himself reflexively.

One of the soldiers, a medic, presented Upshaw with a well-used smartphone. "Picked this up from the pile of sandy stuff over there. Somebody's body dissolved? Got some photos for you."

Upshaw studied the images recorded by the deceased park ranger. He tilted the phone toward Weatherall. "Look at that machine . . ." But Weatherall wasn't paying attention. Down in the pit, another ranger was shedding glassy particles in a spectacular demonstration of starbot technology's limits.

"What the hell . . ."

Over the next ten minutes, the surviving rangers collapsed as well, one after another, and all that remained were empty uniforms spilling out sand. The witnesses peering down into the dig were all bug-eyed with horror.

"Better get down there. See what the starbots were up to," said Weatherall bravely.

▼

A squad of American combat engineers quickly set up a kitchen, porta-potties, tents, and most important, sturdy aluminum ladders for access to the colossal hole in the ground created by the starbots.

What Upshaw, Weatherall, and their team discovered when they descended into the dig site was a labyrinth of stone-walled rooms. Here a possible bathroom with a stone toilet, there a set of stone chairs. On the walls, intricately carved symbols.

"That toilet, those chairs," speculated Weatherall. "They don't look like they were carved with hand tools, or designed for my anatomy."

"Who then?"

"The starbot creators? Maybe they really did show up here, a long time ago."

"How long? These artifacts, the walls, people couldn't build stuff like this until Egypt and the Greeks got going. Everything looks almost new."

Weatherall ran a finger over the carvings. "Alien writing. Does it give you a funny feeling?"

Upshaw shook his head. "After nine-eleven, nothing phases me."

"Come on, Mo. You don't fool me. This place is spooky."

She adjusted the headlight on her hard hat, ducked into a narrow alleyway and led Upshaw into a back room, where they came upon a grisly sight. There, stacked like firewood, were a dozen naked bodies, the human remains of the Great Zimbabwe park rangers.

Weatherall recoiled. "Ughhh . . ."

Upshaw rubbed his chin. "Jim Lockwood was transformed by those damn bushes we were collecting. But that took years. This is something else, another process."

"Yes, involving murder."

Stepping around the bodies, they turned a corner and stumbled upon the sarcophagus recently desecrated by the starbots. Upshaw focused his flashlight on the tomb interior, where leathery material and cartilaginous bone-like objects hinted at the tattered remains of a corpse.

"What — ?"

Weatherall peered closely at the papery tissue. "What, indeed? We have to check the starbots' mythology — how old is this place, these remains?"

She turned her head this way and that to get a better sense of the room.

"And what else is going on? I have the same uneasy feeling I had when I first saw those bushes, back in Tucson."

Upshaw nodded. "Let's get Roman down here. Get our tech guru out of his comfort zone."

"He won't come. He's really bothered by stuff like this."

Upshaw chuckled. "Garibaldi's a scientist. His curiosity will overcome his fear." He raised a finger. "By my order."

▼

Dr. Garibaldi arrived on a small Embraer regional jet from Johannesburg after a sixteen hour commercial flight on Delta.

"They call that cattle car business class. The food was terrible," he griped. "But I prepared by watching the latest *Star Wars* movie twice."

He gestured toward a companion standing behind him, beckoned the man to come forward. "You want my expertise? Here it is — meet Larry Pomeroy. He's a geologist from Brown University."

Upshaw, Weatherall, and Mobanda shook hands with the newcomers.

"And what's your particular specialty, if I may ask, Dr. Pomeroy?" queried Weatherall.

Pomeroy was young and bearded, an assistant professor hoping for tenure. "Ahh, that would be geochronology, dating rocks. Carbon, Potassium, Thorium, you name it. Raman spectroscopy, isotopic ratios, whatever it takes."

He made a casual survey of the dig site, marveling at the precisely carved walls and furniture. Then he turned to the pit's natural boundary, layer upon layer of fine sediment. He ran a finger down through the strata.

"I won't be able to give you an exact date until I get some of this material into the lab. But I can tell you two things already — one, see the layers here? How many of them? The site is very old, probably as old as the human race, and two, in that remote era, who was smart enough to sculpt rock like the examples we see all around us?"

The ITF contingent exchanged glances, held their tongues.

"So . . ." Pomeroy stuck his hands in the pockets of his cargo shorts. He cocked his head. "What am I missing?"

Upshaw showed the geologist photos of the starbot digging machine taken by the park ranger who first encountered it.

Garibaldi peered over Pomeroy's shoulder. "Wow," said he, turning pale.

Weatherall placed a steadying hand on her colleague's arm. "Roman? You okay?"

Garibaldi nodded. "It's not the photos. Not the artifacts. Not the dead park rangers. Something else is creeping me out." He lurched toward one of the rocky chairs and slumped down on it.

"Tell you what — that woman, Sarzeau, the witch. Works for Weaver." He snapped his fingers. "FULTAP, right? She's in camp at the wrecking yard, get her over here. If I notice something, she'll notice it too, maybe give us some answers."

26

MARIANNE SARZEAU, her husband Tom, and their son Gabriel were bivouacked in the charmless Buckeye Oasis Motor Lodge, in tiny Buckeye, Arizona, conveniently situated about twenty miles east of Stone Valley Scrap & Salvage and the starbot base there. They owed the comfort of their home-away-from-home to NITCOM, which had commandeered the entire motel to house more than half of its personnel. It wasn't much, but it was better than one of the army trailers, or worse, one of the tents.

Sarzeau stirred in the early morning hours. She blinked herself awake, rolled onto her back and stared at the ceiling, where the headlights of passing cars and trucks danced with neon bar signs in an evolving abstract art show. She assumed she was troubled by her upcoming assignment to join the NITCOM expedition in Zimbabwe, but then she noticed a small figure leaning on the window sill, staring out into the night.

She leaned over and gave Tom a kiss on his shoulder, then threw the bed covers aside and tiptoed to the window.

"Hey, Gabe, baby, what are you doing up at this hour?"

"Oh hi, Mom. I know you have to go."

"Really. I thought I was keeping a small secret until tomorrow."

"Whiskeyjack told me."

"Oh he did, did he? And when was this?"

"Tonight. I woke up, and he was talking to me."

"You were dreaming, I bet."

"That's not true! I was worried about the starbots, but Whiskeyjack says it's all right. He promised to keep you safe."

Sarzeau frowned. She smoothed Gabe's hair and gently rubbed his back while considering her son's precocious abilities.

"I'm not sure Whiskeyjack can promise anything."

Gabe turned from the window, stretched his arms around Sarzeau's waist, and hugged her tight.

"We will help you, Mom. Don't worry."

"Don't you worry either. Dad's here, and I won't be gone very long."

Gabe pulled back and studied his mother's shadowy face.

"Are all ghosts like Whiskeyjack? He's awfully big. Is he a giant? Does he have, like, ghost guns and stuff?"

Sarzeau bit her lip.

"You know, I don't think Whiskeyjack is a ghost at all."

"But you said . . ."

"I used to think so. That's why I'm a little bit religious, why we go to church."

"But he can walk on air, and he doesn't need a phone."

"Here's what I think — Mr. W is a living being, like us, only from a faraway place, and some of us can talk to him."

"Gee, right through outer space?"

"Right through outer space! It only seems empty. Reality is strange, kiddo" — she tweaked his nose — "and now, back to bed with you."

▼

Sarzeau arrived in Great Zimbabwe National Park after a series of mind-numbing flights from Arizona on three different airlines.

Dr. Garibaldi, with high expectations, and Dr. Pomeroy, with grave doubts, volunteered to give her a tour of the dig site.

"So, um, you're a witch? You sense auras?" inquired Pomeroy. He was awed by the fair-haired woman, whose youthful beauty, even while attired in a work shirt and hard hat, belied her reputation, but he was reluctant to have his belief in the supreme power of science challenged by some New Age chick from the sticks.

Sarzeau turned her golden brown eyes on the geologist.

"Most of the time I'm a local cop in the California foothills. A mom with two kids. On weekends I'm a disc jockey on our local radio station. And now and then, when duty calls, I'm an agent for General Weaver's FULTAP outfit.

"FULTAP? What's that?"

"It's a branch of Defense Intelligence. We do psychic surveillance. My dad got me involved."

Garibaldi smiled. "Her trade name is *Broomhandle.*"

"Is dad like you, some sort of male witch?"

"You mean, warlock? No, nothing so scary. He's the one who can see people's auras, guess their attitudes, gauge intentions."

"But you can cast spells?"

"That's right, I can." She grinned. "Better watch your step, doc, or I'll turn you into an artifact."

Garibaldi halted in front of a low wall, and held up a hand to redirect the discussion.

"Okay, boys and girls. Here's where I get the heebie-jeebies. Right here."

Pomeroy scratched his head. "I don't notice anything."

Sarzeau stood very still facing the wall, on which was engraved an oval symbol of unknown origin. She closed her eyes and let her thoughts drain away.

"Sarzeau? Hello?"

Her eyes snapped open.

"Well, what do you know? I do sense something. It's faint, but it's real. There is a presence behind this wall."

"A presence . . ." Pomeroy was incredulous. "My survey tells me there's nothing here except very old dirt."

Sarzeau was irritated by the conventional skepticism she faced wherever she went, and although she was a headstrong woman who did not suffer fools gladly, she had learned to temper her temper.

"Have you tried ground penetrating radar?" she asked politely.

Pomeroy winced. "We ordered a setup. It's on the next plane."

"Then for now, I guess I'm all you've got. Better put on your face masks."

She tucked her nose into her own mask and waited for her guides to follow her example. Then, with full confidence in her peculiar kind of intuition, she placed her hands on the upper edge of the wall and gave it a hard shove.

The wall cracked and toppled backward, enveloping the trio in a cloud of fine dust. The cloud slowly dissipated, revealing the shadowy geometry of an interior room.

Off came the masks.

"Holy shit," gulped Pomeroy.

He probed the space with a powerful flashlight, then led the way inside.

"Walls. Masonry. Dry. Carved, like the rest of the site. Some water seepage."

He turned his light toward Sarzeau.

"Wow, apology! Sorry to sound like a jerk."

Sarzeau held up a fist. Pomeroy did the same. They bumped. "Apology accepted." She turned her own light on the far wall. "What have we here? A mural . . ."

Beyond a forest of narrow stalagmites formed by groundwater leaking down through the ceiling, an indistinct image was visible. It resembled the DNA signature geneticists had discovered and verified in the human genome. Triangular head, two arms, two long legs.

Garibaldi remained where the wall fell, just a step or two inside the room. "The feeling is worse here. Why don't I get ourselves some work lights."

Sarzeau was impressed by the scientist's anxiety. "Why, Roman, whether you know it or not, you're almost *adept*. Untrained, unskilled, but . . . ever think about it? Something's going on in that technical brain of yours."

Garibaldi threw up his hands. "Ha-ha, that's really funny, Sarzeau. I'll grab our documentation camera, be right back."

Work lights, cameras, spectrum analyzers, X-ray imagers, Dr. Weatherall, and a squad of technicians were all in place within twenty minutes.

Pomeroy broke through the stalagmites with his field hammer, opening the way for a uniformed Army technician to spray the mural with a jet of steam, flaking off a crust of limestone deposited over the eons, bringing the image and its surrounding symbols into sharp relief, and revealing seams that suggested the location of a door.

Lights flashed and shutters clicked to record the discovery.

Garibaldi tapped one of the cameras. "NSA is going to check out our pix. They've got a supercomputer, latest AI, deep mind, neuron tech, decrypts anything in no time."

"Oh?" Pomeroy was used to the heroic efforts of archeologists and scholars who took decades to understand Egyptian and Mayan hieroglyphs.

"You bet. They call it the *Nutcracker.* They read the Russians, the Iranians, and the Chinese like last Sunday's newspaper."

Sarzeau approached the diagram. She ran a hand over the abstract face and arms.

"This isn't the edge of the dig. There's another room."

Pomeroy still harbored doubts. He was examining a rough set of drawings that depicted the dig's mapped extent. "You sure?"

"Yes, I'm sure."

She pushed hard against the suspected door, but failed to budge it.

"Ugh. Something's in here, I can feel it. Brr . . ."

27

U.S. SECRETARY OF STATE Morey Rutledge, looking tall and distinguished, was standing behind a lectern in the main conference room of the Royal Court Hotel in Ramallah, the administrative capital of Palestine. Beside him was a dour Palestinian official, pouring out a diatribe in angry Arabic.

Rutledge waited patiently for the man to finish, then adjusted his microphone to deliver a postmortem on his recent meetings with the Palestinian National Authority.

"The United States, as always, stands ready to aid the cause of Palestine, but regrettably our current efforts to broker a Middle East peace have not succeeded."

He eyed a limousine pulling up outside the window. He was hoping to get away, and the sooner the better.

"Terms have been discussed, and we have made considerable progress, but roadblocks remain, and positive results, I'm sorry to say, are not in view at this time."

The room was full of reporters from all over the world. A hand shot up, and Ian Gilmore, none other than Nikki Traeger's source of information on the starbots' remote location, posed a question.

"Mr. Secretary, dealing with the Middle East and its factions is a difficult matter. I know you were one of the brave souls on the starbot tour in Arizona, and I wonder if you could enlighten us on what looks like a far more difficult diplomatic mission — a mission with galactic consequences. What are the starbots doing here on Earth? Are they a threat? Are negotiations underway? Will you play a part in resolving the situation?"

Rutledge held up his hands in a gesture of helplessness. "Threat? The real threat we face is right here on Earth, man against man."

He fingered his tie.

"Bloodshed has dogged the human race since we learned to walk upright. Our dark side, original sin. Perhaps we should cede our authority to the starbots. Our security could hardly be worse. Why not? Let them arbitrate our squabbles, police our ambitions, relieve us of our woes. As old Hobbes so wisely put it, commission a Leviathan to rule over us and 'keep us all in awe.'"

Gilmore was dumbfounded by the Secretary's answer. "Are you serious? Some people would rebel, don't you think?"

Rutledge was tired, he was frustrated, he was filled with gloom.

"Perfectly serious. We don't know if the starbots plan to remain with us indefinitely or not. Looking to them for guidance, it's a proposal that has some merit, I believe. It should be closely examined."

▼

"He said *what?*"

U.S. President Porter Fairbanks was in the middle of a cabinet meeting in the White House when word of Secretary Rutledge's remarks reached his ears. His rugged countenance turned red, contrasting sharply with his steel-grey hair.

"Allow me to explain, Mr. President." Before he was appointed Secretary of the Interior, the bringer of bad news was Fairbanks' campaign manager. He shrank from the political danger of igniting presidential wrath. "The Secretary was replying to an interview question following the Palestinian fiasco. Provoked into his response, really. He didn't get much sleep the night before . . ."

Fairbanks was sixty-five years old, a tough ex-marine, a former prosecuting attorney, and the previous governor of Ohio.

"I don't give a good goddamn if the man spent the night screwing Palestinian whores. This is not a message I want to send."

"No, sir, it's not."

"The country is looking to us — to *me!* — to master this crisis, keep America safe." He brought bushy eyebrows together in a deep frown. "We are taking charge, not the fucking starbots. Everyone got that?"

A chorus: "Yes, sir."

"And America needs to know we are on top of the situation, got the problem under control."

A new voice piped up from the far end of the table. "Yes, sir, of course, that's number one. But, if I may?"

The President focused on the speaker, who appeared to be offering a challenge to his authority. He wasn't completely fluent with his cabinet members' names in the best of times, and never with the identity of his appointees' assistants.

"Who's that? What?"

"It's Michaelson, sir. I work for Commerce. Rutledge, the Aussie PM, they're right, you know. Aside from the workers, no sign of hostility. Technically, they're way beyond us, have a lot to offer. Wise to prep for trouble, but let's not start it, Mr. President."

Emboldened by this opinion, the Secretary of Defense offered his own assessment.

"General Congreve is top hat, Mr. President, best man for the job, no confusion there. Sooner or later I think he will be forced to act. Our problem is intent — I'm thinking history, when Cortez paid a visit to the Aztecs. He was with them for quite a while before relations soured."

The President glared. "Today we're writing our own history, Douglas. What's your point?"

"There's a parallel here, as others have noticed. When things finally did go off the rails, his little band destroyed an empire. Pizarro down in Peru with the Incas? Same thing. I'm just saying, beware the Cortez strategy."

The President nodded. "Duly noted. I share the concern. Nevertheless, words before deeds. America needs a positive nudge. Up their confidence in their leaders" — he spread his arms out inclusively — "That's us, a bunch of morons who have no idea what's really going on."

▼

That evening, President Fairbanks addressed the nation from his desk in the Oval Office on five TV networks.

"My fellow Americans, we live in uncertain times. We may be on the verge of joining a galactic society, or facing bloody war. I have never tried to fool you, and I value your trust and your good sense too much to try to fool you now.

"The starbots pose a challenge — to our ingenuity and to our diplomacy. Accordingly, I am making several adjustments in my administration out of an abundance of caution, in order to focus closely on whatever the future holds.

"Secretary of State Rutledge has resigned, effective immediately, with my thanks for his service. His replacement is what the current moment demands, my National Security Advisor, Walter Melrose. His assistant, Bernard Wyatt, already on the ground at the starbot base in Arizona, is perfectly positioned to take over his former post. Other changes may follow.

"I can't tell you how the situation with our unusual visitors will develop. This much I do know — one way or another, we will prevail, and the way we choose to live our lives, the American way, will not be compromised.

"Good night, and God bless us all."

28

TOM WAGSTAFF was bored. His son Gabriel was bored. While Sarzeau was away on her official duties, the pair strained to find ways to entertain themselves. Tom, the journalist, was always on the lookout for a story, something offbeat that he could claim as his own, instead of the mass coverage provided by the TV networks and newspapers. Gabe, thrilled by the prospect of actual aliens, just wanted some adventure.

They got their wishes by hiking around the perimeter of Stone Valley Scrap & Salvage whenever the military patrols let up. Tom wrote an article about the small rat-like robots that scooted in and out of the wrecked vehicles, carrying away small hunks of wire, an occasional car radio, rubber weather seals, and swatches of upholstery. Gabe discovered a hole in the perimeter fence.

"Does Whiskeyjack talk to you?" inquired Gabe, during one of their outings.

"No, just your Mom, and not very often. Why?"

"We talk a lot. I'm going to be his assistant."

"Is that so?"

"Yeah, he needs some help."

"From you?"

"Yeah. We're friends. He likes me."

"I'll bet he does. I like you too, you know."

Tom was alarmed by his young son's supernatural abilities. He was pretty well convinced that Whiskeyjack wasn't just an imaginary friend, but he didn't think a monster's friendship was healthy for a second grader, and he resented the intrusion into his family life.

"Be careful with your pal, Gabe. He's just as strange as the starbots."

"We have a plan. Don't worry, Dad, I will be alright."

Tom bent down on one knee and looked Gabe in the eye. "What did you say?"

"Whiskeyjack gave me a mission. It will be awesome."

"Listen, buddy, and think. How do we know that Whiskeyjack isn't one of *them?* A starbot trying to fool you."

"He's not one of them. He is Whiskeyjack."

"Let's ask Mom when she gets back. She knows him a lot better than you do."

Gabe leaned close and gave Dad a big hug.

"I'm going to be an agent, like Mom. You'll see."

Suddenly, Gabe turned and ran away. Tom lurched to his feet and took off after him.

"Get back here, Gabe. Stop! Get back here this instant!"

But Gabriel had a good head start, and by the time Tom got his feet moving, his son had already reached the hole in the fence he had previously discovered and crawled through it.

The hole was much too small for Tom's adult bulk. He stuck his fingers through the mesh and furiously rattled the chain links.

"Gabriel Sarzeau Wagstaff! Get yourself back here right now! Hear me!? No joke, kid! Right now!"

▼

Wagstaff banged on the NITCOM command post and stormed inside to report his son's terrifying disappearance and beg for help.

"I'm sorry, Mr. Wagstaff. This is a grim development, it will weigh on our security choices going forward, but at the moment there is very little we can do."

Wagstaff acknowledged the rebuff with a sad shrug, and shambled away. He was sure that the mission managers gave him the cold shoulder because they had no idea how to handle the starbots. Feckless wimps, all of them! Waiting for information on the starbot ship and its doings in Africa. That, and word from the President.

His thoughts were whirling out of control, and he hardly knew what to do, but soon he was back at the wrecking yard perimeter.

"James Lockwood! Come out and talk to me, you bastard. Bring me my son!"

The Lockwood transform did not appear, and instead Director Brom-Kat-Su floated out to the fence on his hoverboard. At the same moment, members of NITCOM's patrol unit rushed up to collar the unruly journalist before he started an interstellar war.

"Mr. Wagstaff, step away from the fence, sir."

"Fuck you. My son's in there!" He turned to the starbot. "Yo, Brom! — that's you, right? The bot in charge! — where's Gabe? Don't you dare harm a hair on his head. He belongs to me, my wife and me."

Brom-Kat-Su boomed out his response in robotic tones. "Do not worry. You're son is safe with us."

One of the soldiers attempted to guide Wagstaff away from the fence. The distraught parent shook him off.

"Safe? He won't be safe until you give him back."

Wagstaff wondered if the shiny robot was secretly rolling his many eyes, because Big Brom stood motionless, oblivious to his desperate plea.

"You desire your son," granted the starbot. "And we desire peace and tranquility. We see the guns, we hear the calls to action. Against that background, for now the child must remain with us," he decreed. "Our hostage."

Two of the soldiers grasped Wagstaff around his shoulders and forcibly dragged him away from the confrontation.

"Let me go! They've got my son!"

"Gotta quit while you're ahead, sir."

"Arrrhh . . . you sound like them, like the fucking bots!"

"That's enough. We could have shot you. Thank your lucky stars we didn't."

▼

Wagstaff bided his time until nightfall. Then he loitered around the pen NITCOM had set up to corral journalists whenever Lockwood and the august Brom-Kat-Su appeared for announcements or deigned to grant an interview.

He watched the soldiers on patrol, observed their patterns. When he was sure they were out of his way, he moseyed along the perimeter until he came to Gabriel's hole in the fence.

He was carrying a blanket from his motel in a small backpack. Now he removed it, folded it in quarters, and hung it over the razor wire NITCOM combat engineers had installed on top of the fence itself. Then he hoisted himself up and over.

He was inside, on starbot grounds.

He moved slowly toward the Quonset hut that served as the center of starbot operations, picking his way through the derelict remains of American transportation's golden age.

He was making good progress when he heard the noise of scuttling feet. Aha, the starbots had their own patrols, and something was coming his way. He looked around for a place to hide. The only decent option was a late model Ford Taurus that had suffered fatal front end damage. He pried the driver's door open, slid inside, and managed to pull the door nearly closed just before a many-legged robot that looked like a spider closed in.

He thought he was busted, but the thing passed right on by.

As he sat in the car, wiping away cobwebs, he began to think about his adventure, its purpose, its very low probability of success. He wasn't even sure what success meant. Rescue Gabe? Of course. Show his determination to the starbots, make an appeal, get them to understand something about family bonds of affection? Why not? His cause was noble. Or maybe he could force the issue with his fellow men, provoke a fight when NITCOM discovered he was captured too and realized the starbots were heartless monsters.

Maybe . . . however, the more he thought about it, the less he thought of his prospects. He stared out through the ruined car's windshield at the Quonset hut, still far away. "You are a hopeless jerk," he told his crazed reflection, muttering aloud. "And a terrible parent, don't forget. What makes you think this suicide mission atones for your sad fuck-ups?"

But the scuttling sound faded away, and the coast cleared. His mood rebounded. "Hey, that thing walked right by. Missed me completely."

He had considered the starbots to be superior beings because their technology was so advanced, but now he revised his estimation. Maybe they weren't so smart. Maybe it had taken them long centuries to acquire their technical prowess. Maybe they envied humanity's facile creativity.

"We humans, hah! Clever bastards! Quick! Alert! Try and stop us!"

With his self esteem thus buoyed, he got out of the car and resumed his quest. Fifty yards to the Quonset hut. Edging past a rusty Datsun pickup truck. Thirty yards. Scrambling over the hood of a Chevy Bel-Air wedged tightly against the hulk of a Chrysler Imperial. Twenty yards. Squirming past a tiny Fiat 500 that met an early death. Ten yards.

He rounded a corner and stood in the doorway of the hut. Inside he could see several bots working on alien machinery under bright lights.

"Well, hello, fellas. Here I am. I want my son back."

Phase **4**

29

LOOK HERE, when I clean them up, we see the symbols are arranged in order of complexity. Numbers?"

Larry Pomeroy was brushing dust off the mural in the ancient room that Sarzeau opened up within the starbot dig site in Great Zimbabwe National Park.

Dr. Garibaldi stroked his chin. "I swear we've got a door here, right in front of us, but I don't see anything like a knob or locks, or latches."

Weatherall was parked nearby in a canvas chair. She rose and ran a finger over the obscure symbols etched into the wall surface. "Eight symbols in all, could be octal math. Puzzle, you think?"

Sarzeau stood by with arms folded. "Sure, an ancient combination lock!"

Pomeroy exhaled through his teeth. "And we don't have the combination."

"Even if we did, after all this time, the mechanism will never work."

Pomeroy nodded. "Violating every academic prohibition against destroying archeological sites, to say nothing of my conscience, I've asked for crowbars, wedges, sledge hammers." He grinned sheepishly. "Don't tell my dean at Brown, I'll lose tenure."

Soon enough, a soldier appeared with an entrenching tool and a wrench meant for aircraft maintenance. Using the wrench as a hammer, Pomeroy banged the blade into one of the seams in the mural and pried with all his might. The handle gave way, bending sideways, but the door — if it was a door — did not budge.

"Well, shit."

The group was suddenly illuminated by a series of bright flashes. they turned toward the source, and there was Nikki

Traeger, blasting them with a strobe light on her Nikon.

"Hey, stop that!"

Traeger lowered the camera. "It's okay, I'm documenting."

"Beg pardon — ?"

"Oh, I know you have photometric tools, your science gadgets, but this is also news, big news. Think about it! TV, headlines in every paper, viral on the web, then magazine covers, and after that the history books — posterity!"

"Look, you're off limits. How did you find us, anyway?" wondered Garibaldi. He was irritated by the reporter's easy manner. "How did you get here?"

"Uncle Sam's C-130."

Pomeroy brightened. "Did you see a radar set on the plane?"

"Not sure. All I saw was me, and a year's supply of meals-ready-to-eat."

The group stared at her with mouths agape.

Traeger clocked the residual hostility. She reached into a pocket of her photographer's vest and showed off a formal note on NIT-COM stationery. "To whom it may concern, people. I'm authorized to be here by General Congreve."

Garibaldi snatched the sheet of paper and examined it. "Embedded? How? Did you hypnotize the man?"

Traeger grinned. "Guess who located the starbot landing site, where you are now hard at work. I made a deal for the info."

"You're kidding," blurted Sarzeau.

"No, honey, I'm not. Hey, all of you stand over there by those carvings, it's a great shot!"

Nobody moved. Traeger squinted at the mural. "Is that a door? What's on the other side?"

Sarzeau sighed. "We don't know. It's a puzzle."

Traeger took a closer look. "Oh, a puzzle. Looks tough." She waved a hand. "Damn, before I forget, which one of you is

Sarzeau?"

Sarzeau nodded.

Traeger took her by the arm and pulled her aside.

"I'm sorry about this, hate to be the one to bring bad news . . ."

Sarzeau froze.

". . . but your son and your husband have been captured by the starbots."

"Oh my God!"

"They've stashed your family somewhere inside that Quonset hut. Hostages against military action."

"No, no, no . . ."

"It's okay, they're safe. No good to the bots if they're dead."

Sarzeau whirled around. "I've got to get back there. Gotta help them. Where's your plane? Did it take off?" She bolted toward the open pit.

Garibaldi intercepted her. "Hang on, Marianne. You can't go. We need you here."

"Out of my way, Roman."

"Think, woman. The starbots were here, dug the hole we're in, and found — nothing. They've got their technology, but we've got you. Our secret weapon."

"Oh, man . . ."

"We need your crazy superpowers. They're vital."

Sarzeau dug in her heels, came to a stop. Her mind was spinning.

"Get me a mirror."

One of the soldiers provided a mirror the troops used for shaving. Sarzeau carried it into a corner of the dig. Weatherall and Garibaldi trailed along behind. She held up a hand to warn them away. Then she hauled out her stony amulet and the acorn Gabriel found in the woods above Applefield. She shook them at the mirror.

"Whiskeyjack! You bastard, you did this! You better talk to me, better have a damn good story to tell!"

The mirror reflected her face, where tears were starting to form. She bit her lip, forced herself to remain calm, wait for her other-worldly contact's arrival. But nothing happened for more than a minute. It seemed like eternity, so she resorted to her cruder summoning method . . .

"Whiskeyjack?! Hey, you!"

Another minute went by, and she was near despair. But then the mirror darkened. A smoky figure loomed into view. Electric blue eyes peered out at her

Marianne. Far away, hard to find. How may I be of service?

"Don't be so damn polite! You got Tom and Gabriel captured by the starbots."

I did. Guilty as charged.

"What if they get transformed? Huh? What if? You did this, and you have to undo it. Have to get them out of danger."

They are not in danger. They are safe. I am watching over them.

"How do you know? You're living on some astral plane, and we're all stuck here on Earth. Stuck with the starbots."

They will not be harmed. They have work to do.

"Oh great. We've seen the wrecking yard workers, and they aren't human anymore."

You must trust me. Trust me and go about your business. You too have work to do.

"A lot of help you are!"

My humble best.

Sarzeau was readying a retort when the smoky figure faded from view. She made to smash the mirror on the ground, but an anxious soldier snatched it out of her hands.

"Sheesh, lady, be careful with that."

30

HOLLY CHOW and Guy Holzgraf felt useless hanging around Stone Valley Scrap & Salvage, and so, a day after Sarzeau departed for Zimbabwe, they flew back to Tucson in his little Robinson helicopter. Although the Australian Prime Minister, the U.S. President, his former Secretary of State, and other officials counseled forbearance, they were both filled with misgivings about the starbots, worried that a battle was coming, worried that explosive devices were going to kill a lot of people.

They preferred the silent operation of their refined microwave gun, and they were hoping to modify its design to overcome the starbots' countermeasures.

Within the walls of Darlington Energetix, all thoughts of advanced solar panels and artificial photosynthesis were banished in favor of microwave lasers.

"Look, here in the catalog — the lasers are tunable," noted Holly.

"Great, focused power without a twenty-pound battery."

Holzgraf was studying graphs on his laptop.

"Our problem — it might be where the signals cross. The downsweep always crosses the upsweep at the same wavelength."

Chow was facing him across a shared desk, elbows planted, propping up her chin with her fists.

"What if it's all a crude form of encryption?"

"How would that work?"

"Well, once upon a time we could zap these things, and now we can't. I don't think the bots could completely re-engineer everything that makes them tick, do you?"

"Now that you mention it . . ."

"Then — they just changed a code, a code that they use to assemble and break down their own stuff."

"And we need to figure out their code." Holzgraf sighed. "It will be so easy."

Chow grimaced. "Yeah . . . but wait, why not force our gun to sample all the crossing frequencies."

"And while it's doing that, they kill us instead."

"We could do the sweeps really fast."

▼

At the wrecking yard, Captain Hugh Donaldson, lately recovered from wounds received in the infamous starbot assault that captured one of NITCOM's original wave guns, was on the perimeter, wrangling a squad of Rangers.

Under his direction, soldiers excavated the ground under a section of the fence and deposited shreds of aluminum foil in the resulting trench. Then they waited.

Pretty soon one of the crab-like, crab-sized starbots scuttled over to check things out. It eyed the aluminum foil and reached out with one of its front claws to grab it.

Donaldson thrust out a pole with a snare on the end like the ones desert dwellers use to collect rattlesnakes. He lassoed the thing and dropped it into a carbon fiber bag.

A few hours later he presented it to Chow and Holzgraf in their Tucson laboratory, where the pair had built a pen out of steel rods and heavy acrylic plastic sheets.

"Okay, Hugh, turn it loose!" called Holzgraf.

Donaldson dumped the diminutive robot into the specially constructed enclosure, where it ran around the border, frantically trying to escape. Chow readied her newly revised weapon and squeezed the trigger. A microwave laser beam stabbed out to test the starbot's vulnerability.

"Oh, crap."

The little creature didn't even slow down.

31

SARZEAU couldn't sleep.

In the middle of the night she rose from her tent in the NIT-COM military encampment and wandered around the Zimbabwe Great Enclosure, marveling at the fine stone masonry, imagining the people who, centuries ago, went to such heroic lengths to construct a monument.

"Monument to what?" she mused aloud.

"Not a clue," came a voice. It startled her. She spun around and there was Garibaldi, gesturing toward the conical tower that dominated the park.

"Oh, hey, Roman, you can't sleep either," said she.

"Mmm, no, I got stuck thinking about our door puzzle."

"What about the NSA and their supercomputer?"

"The *Nutcracker* is cracked, but the puzzle is not. Message came through an hour ago — *unable to decrypt submitted text.*"

"So much for human technology."

Sarzeau spread her arms wide to take in the entire park. "Ever think about inspiration? Why, do you suppose, did the Shona ancestors choose this place to build their palace, temple, whatever it was?"

"That's one for the archeologists. Maybe Larry has an idea, I don't."

"I think they felt something here."

"Possible, I guess."

"And — I still feel it. You do too when we get inside that room."

"I try not to think too hard about that."

"Right — I don't blame you. Ever visit Chaco Canyon? Or Mesa Verde?"

"Nope."

"Tom and I have. Road trip. Ancient Anasazi Indian sites, about the same age as this place. Know what? While I was there I didn't feel a thing."

"Your point?"

"I don't feel history, don't feel the dear departed. I feel the here and now. And I feel a *presence*. Something is still putting out energy."

"After a couple of hundred thousand years? Don't be silly."

"Who's being silly? You're the hairy ape telling interstellar travelers what they can and cannot do."

"Arf," barked Garibaldi, cheerfully acknowledging his human arrogance.

Sarzeau looked up into the sky. Little diamond-hard pinpoints of light were strewn across the deep dark heavens over Africa.

"Biological aliens got here somehow — the DNA proof, right? What were they thinking about? Why make the trip?"

"Weatherall and her gang figured out that their home planet has no air," speculated the scientist. "Maybe it ran out. Maybe they were looking for airy real estate."

"You mean, location, location, location."

"Right. Or, how about this — our visitors were a cult, a religious group, like the Pilgrims in America, four hundred years ago. Not official representatives of their planet, just crazies filled with big ideas about galactic brotherhood."

"And the starbots? What do you make of them?"

Garibaldi pursed his lips. "I guess they don't need air, so they outlived their creators."

The African night was cool. Sarzeau folded her arms to ward off a sudden chill.

"And then they evolved on their own?"

"Seems likely."

Sarzeau grimaced. "Why does that bother me?"

Multiple flashes of a camera strobe light caught Garibaldi's eye, interrupting the conversation. He started off toward their recently discovered underground room.

"Whoa, there! Somebody's in our dig site, Sarzeau."

That somebody was Nikki Traeger, documenting the mural with her Nikon.

"Hey, lady, who gave you permission to sneak into our site?"

Traeger looked up from adjusting a reflector panel and its slave strobe. She smiled.

"Busted."

"What do you think you're doing?"

"Shooting your mural with decent lighting. It will be a knockout on the cover of Time Magazine."

"Too bad we haven't solved the puzzle, see what's inside."

Traeger stared at the mural. "All the symbols are kind of curly, see, all except this rectangle here. Gotta represent the door."

"Hmm. We tried pushing on it."

"How tough can it be? Two hundred thousand years ago, who did the aliens have to fool? *Monkeys.*"

They waited until morning, when Pomeroy and Weatherall woke up and joined them.

Encouraged by Traeger's assessment, Sarzeau pursued an idea she was hatching. On close inspection, one arm of the alien depicted in the mural ended in a slight depression. Sarzeau leaned forward and stretched out her own arms. She pressed the fingers of one hand against the end of the alien arm and the fingers of her other hand against the rectangular symbol that might represent their firmly closed door. Then she stepped back.

Ka-thunk

A dull noise and a slight tremor made Sarzeau's heart skip a beat. A fine spray of dust blew out of the seam that separated mural from possible door.

"Face masks on, everyone."

Sarzeau gave it a push, but nothing happened, the hoped-for door did not open.

"Damn."

Pomeroy reared back and gave the putative door a good kick.

"I studied Taekwondo. Wasted years, black belt, et cetera," he explained.

The door creaked inward an inch or so.

The group shuffled forward in anticipation.

Sarzeau held up a hand. She wiggled her fingers.

"Here's what I think . . ."

She reached out and gingerly touched each of the curly symbols in left-to-right order.

"Open sesame, please!" said she, mocking herself and her feeble attempt.

But another tremor and a low rumble caused everyone to edge backward as the door obliged by rotating away on invisible hinges, raising a cloud of ancient dust, expelling a bubble of fetid air, and revealing yet another chamber in the alien habitation.

32

GENERAL CONGREVE was on the phone to the early warning team in their mountain hideaway at NORAD.

"What do you mean, 'contact unverified'?"

Pause.

"We know the bots have left Zimbabwe."

Pause.

"How? Because that's where my away team is right now. What I want to know is, what's their next target?"

Pause.

"You're unable to say, and I'm unable to say, and this is a clusterfuck. We need to know what's going on."

Pause.

"Fine. I await a call at your early convenience."

Congreve slammed his phone down.

"Son of a bitch!"

General Upshaw, General Weaver, Acting Secretary of State Melrose, and Barney Wyatt, now the President's designated National Security Advisor, stared at their commander, whose face was almost purple with outraged frustration.

"Our pals at NORAD surmise that the starbots have 'very effective stealth technology.'" Congreve ran a hand through his hair. "I'll say!"

His four associates lapsed into silent thought, unwilling to stir Congreve's wrath with any comments.

While they all fumed, the sergeant responsible for NITCOM surveillance knocked on the command post door and let himself in. He was breathless with excitement.

"Excuse me, um, something you all should see . . ."

He opened up a laptop he was carrying and started a video clip.

"Cameras 1 and 5 were focused on the Quonset hut last night.

Look closely, it goes by quick, and my guys on duty didn't pick it up. I was reviewing just now and got lucky."

On the screen the Quonset hut bloomed in the bright lights surrounding the wrecking yard.

"Okay, coming up, that hole in the roof opens . . ."

The group watched a roof panel slide aside, creating a large opening. Light streamed out into the night sky.

"Then, the blur . . ."

Suddenly a large object dropped into the hole, moving so fast that it was just a smear through a single video frame. Then the roof panel slid back into place, cutting off the light.

"What time was this, Sergeant?"

"Oh-four-thirty, sir."

"See it again . . ?"

The non-com ran the clip again.

"So, the ship is back. And no radar signature worth the mention. Very impressive. What next?"

The non-com shifted his weight around. "I got calls from Tonopah, and Wintersburg, and Buckeye. They all report power brownouts from oh-four-hundred hours."

"We can quiz that sando Lockwood — the imperial Lockbot — see what he has to say for himself."

"Locked-lip-bot, you mean. We won't learn a thing."

Barney Wyatt looked up from his third run through the video clip. "Zimbabwe, a World Heritage monument. Think — one of those headline locations. That ship is refueling or something. Bet you it's going to fly again. Question is, Where? How about Valley of the Kings? The tomb of that emperor Qin something, in China? Angkor Wat in Cambodia, et cetera, et cetera."

Congreve nodded. "I hear our team has found something in Africa. We need to get them on the hump as soon as they finish over there."

33

HARD HATS on? Masks on? Okay, troops, let's take a look."
Pomeroy lit his headlamp and led Sarzeau, Traeger, Weatherall, and Garibaldi into their newly discovered room beneath the grassy fields and the stone walls of Great Zimbabwe National Park.

Where the walls of the outer rooms were carved stone masonry, here the walls were flat, smooth, and composed of what looked like some sort of plaster. Pomeroy chipped away a small section, revealing nothing more substantial under the coating than heavy red clay.

In the middle of the room stood a table. Instead of stone, it appeared to be grey plastic.

"This thing. Polymer? It looks like something we might make with a 3D printer."

"Maybe those guys had one with them," speculated Garibaldi.

A metal arm with joints and elbows was standing at one corner of the table, poised over the surface.

A row of shelves and cabinets was built into the far wall, lined with objects that looked like plastic jars. Some of them contained the salty residue of unknown reagents. Set among them were small metal instruments that might have been of medical use.

One wall was covered with peculiar diagrams and cryptic symbols.

Traeger began taking photos. "Ever see anything like this before, doc?"

Pomeroy shook his head in wonderment.

"I see plenty of decay, evidence of great age, but hey, this tops King Tut's tomb."

"May I quote you on that?" grinned Traeger. She was reaching for one of the metal objects.

"You certainly may."

He shot out a hand to deflect Traeger's fingers, accidentally knocking the instrument to the floor, where it shattered.

"But don't touch anything! Anything else, anyway! Jesus! This room is a gold mine. We'll be studying it for years."

Garibaldi cautiously picked up the pieces.

"Be it known — whatever broke was fragile, brittle, old I guess, but this is important — not sand."

Weatherall fingered one of the shards. "Not made by starbots."

Sarzeau studied the room's surprisingly modern artifacts. "This is great," she announced. "Now we know something we've been guessing at."

"And what is that?"

"The starbots aren't too bright. Finding this room — it's a laboratory, right? — proves it. All this was right under their noses. Well, if they had noses. And they couldn't figure it out. Gave up and left. Brains — that's our edge, if it comes to trouble."

Pomeroy allowed a few moments for Traeger to finish her photographic survey, then motioned everyone out of the room.

"We need to establish an investigative protocol, or we'll ruin the site," said he.

They were leaving when a tiny noise turned them around.

"What was that?"

"What was what?"

"That sound."

"I didn't hear anything."

"There it is again."

"Where?"

"Right over there — squeaking noises, like a mouse."

Sarzeau edged back into the room, then recoiled when a silvery robot the size and shape of a cracker box tumbled out of a compartment under the central table and tottered toward her on its only appendages, a pair of spindly legs.

"Ohmigod!"

They all backed into the outer room, followed by the robot. A red laser was flashing on its torso, and the thing was making a variety of strange noises, some pitched high, some low; here and there muttering a recognizable consonant, oohing a vowel or two.

"Good lord," said Pomeroy. "It's trying to talk."

But not for long. Within a few seconds the noises stopped. The red light blinked and went out. The robot stood in place for another moment, then keeled over.

Traeger took photos, documenting the odd little mechanical creature and its silvery parts.

"This is the presence I feel. This little guy," said Sarzeau.

▼

Pomeroy requisitioned a cargo pallet. They carefully lifted the small robot onto the rough wooden platform and carried the thing outside to prepare it for further examination.

While Garibaldi made a satellite call to report the team's sensational find to NITCOM HQ, the Sun came around the eastern hills and illuminated the thing.

Within fifteen minutes, the robot that was presumed dead for two hundred thousand years had sprouted an array of fronds terminating in metallic leaflike structures.

"Hey, everybody — photosynthesis!"

The group gathered round. In another fifteen minutes the robot sat up. Eye stalks grew out of its body and looked around.

"Hey, there, little sneak, who are you? Got a name?"

The robot remained silent for a long minute. Then it chirped a response: "Name? Name? Name?"

Weatherall reeled backward. "Holy crap, it's learning our lingo."

34

BARNEY WYATT was texting back and forth to senior agents at the National Security Agency outside Baltimore.

"When to expect clear text of bot code?" he wrote.

Somebody named Ufford replied obliquely: "Nutcracker no crack nut. Outlook doubtful."

Wyatt showed the text to General Congreve. "So much for our spook tech, General."

"And those bozos are proud of spending a billion dollars on their code-cracking gear," groused Congreve.

"Works with the Russians, sir."

"I'm not too worried about our fellow humans, Barney."

General Weaver returned from a trip to the portable toilets waving his mobile phone in high excitement.

"Gentlemen, those alien symbols —"

"— are not translatable, Vern, we know. We're screwed."

Weaver chuckled. "You boys are obviously starved for news. The ITF group out there in Africa have caught themselves a real live robot."

"As if we needed more," fumed Wyatt.

"This one's different. Made by biological aliens, thousands of years ago, not the starbots."

"And the punch line — ?"

"It can talk."

▼

Yes it could. For a while, anyway.

Garibaldi spent an entire day and night talking to the robot.

"What are you doing?" probed Traeger.

The scientist wiped his brow. "Teaching English. Sentences, vocabulary, grammatical constructions."

"Oh, good to know, because the rest of us thought you might

have lost your mind."

"Maybe I have," he sighed.

But no. Twenty-four hours later, to his and his colleagues' astonishment, the NITCOM team was rewarded with a conversational partner from another world.

"Who are you?"

"Who are you?" repeated the robot.

"No, no, it's not a lesson, it's a question — who made you, where do you come from?"

The red laser flashed from the robot's torso and scanned the surrounding faces, all of them agog with curiosity.

"You be progeny," it decided.

"I guess our DNA proves that, huh? But what about you? Got a name?"

"No name."

Sarzeau bent close. "When those bushes made a robot, Holly called it *Dasher*. Maybe we should call you *Blitzen* or something." She peered at the robot's red laser lens. "Or better yet, *Rudolph*."

Garibaldi smiled. "Okay, Rudy-Red-Nose, what's your job, your purpose?"

"I serve my Lords."

"The aliens?"

"Those who travel here."

"Well, where are they now? We'd like to have a little chat."

"Lords not talk. Gone. All dead."

"We did find a tomb. But only one."

"Lords travel far away. Avoid to live and die with dull, lesser — *annnxxxx.*"

"Lesser? Dull? You mean *inferior?*"

"cruel animals — *annxx* — not worthy."

Garibaldi looked at his fellows. He gestured toward the robot, encouraging questions.

Sarzeau squatted down before the bot. She reached out and touched it. "So . . . tell us, what were your Lords doing here? What brought them to Earth, our planet?"

"Build new world."

"Whoa," interjected Weatherall, "that's a big project. Why would they try?"

"Planet is perfect — *annxx* — almost perfect. Could be perfect."

"Were the Lords planning to settle here permanently?"

"*Annnxxxx . . .*"

The little robot fell backward without offering a clear answer. Weatherall set him back on his haunches. Garibaldi repeated the question several times, but the robot was either sleeping or low on power.

"Damn, we need to know this stuff."

They poked and prodded.

"Think he's dead?"

"At two hundred thousand years, he was powered by a very old battery."

"R-I-P then . . ."

"We could do an autopsy, see what his circuits look like," suggested Garibaldi.

"Jesus, Roman."

"We will do no such thing. He may wake up," insisted Weatherall.

But all attempts to revive the little guy without tearing him apart failed.

Sarzeau returned to what she thought of as the laboratory and patrolled slowly back and forth, searching her supernatural radar for evidence of any more alien surprises. Traeger tagged along with her camera clicking.

"I don't feel a presence now. All is calm."

Traeger pointed to the inner wall, where dry plaster had started to crumble. "Do I see a seam?"

Sarzeau scowled. She dragged a finger over the flaw in the plaster. Little bits fell away, and sure enough, the outlines of a door appeared.

Traeger didn't wait for permission — she pushed. The door rotated a few degrees, then ground to a halt.

"Hey, Larry? Nancy? Roman? Get in here!"

Pomeroy ordered masks and hardhats in place, then used his Taekwondo kick to bang the door all the way open. When the dust cleared, an inky black interior was yawning before the team.

"I'm not going in there," said Garibaldi.

"Come on, Roman, we've got ourselves a major discovery, what we work all our lives for."

"What if there are spiders? Or snakes?"

Traeger snorted, reached into the darkness, and clicked off half a dozen flash photos.

The group studied the digital result on her Nikon's little viewscreen.

"More murals, diagrams."

"A tomb under construction, but abandoned, looks like."

"No body."

"Nope. But there's an illustration on the wall. One of them."

Sarzeau was intrigued by the pictorial aesthetics. "You know, the alien image there. It looks . . . Mexican . . . or maybe Chinese."

Pomeroy shrugged. "Hard to tell. Some do see a similarity between the two visual styles."

Traeger tossed her hair and laughed. "Who cares? No human beings lived in Mexico or China or anywhere else way back when."

35

NITCOM'S away team gathered their gear and their archeological discoveries, packed everything up, and withdrew to Masvingo's tiny airport and three idling C-130Js.

Garibaldi's plan was to send the archeological material, including the little alien robot, back to Arizona, while the team itself moved on to China.

Weatherall wasn't too sure about the idea. "What's in China, Roman? And where?"

"I was just on the horn to Upshaw. Mo says that the starbot ship returned briefly to Stone Valley, then took off again. NORAD has not been able to track the damn thing, but Barney Wyatt has this theory about world class headline locations."

He went on to describe how Wyatt had been sending diplomats and embassy employees to every famous spot on Earth, and how his gamble paid off at the tomb of Qin Shi Huangdi, China's first emperor, just outside the city of Xi'an.

"The bots are digging up the pyramid there, and the Chinese are beside themselves."

"Okay. China it is."

But when they arrived at the airport and were getting ready to strap into one of the cargo planes, Sarzeau refused.

"Sorry, folks, I'm not going with you."

Garibaldi did not take her announcement gracefully. "You have to come. It's absolutely essential. For the good of the Country. Good of humanity, for Christ's sake. It's an order, really."

Sarzeau was adamant.

"Don't mess with me, Roman. Track down my father — he's already out there, I bet, and in case you missed it, he's an adept too. You'll be in good hands."

"Marianne . . ."

"Me? I'm going to get my family out of that Quonset hut."

▼

Nikki Traeger had other plans too. She expressed mild interest in the China operation, but wanted to see a friend in nearby South Africa on the way.

"Old guy, death's door. Taught me how to be a journalist when I was a nasty kid. This is my chance to say goodbye."

The group thanked her for her help and wished her well.

When they were all safely airborne in their Air Force C-130, Traeger booked a series of commercial flights to carry her out of Africa and back across the Atlantic Ocean to Mexico.

36

GUY HOLZGRAF was obsessed by the microwave weapon he and Chow had developed, and he was tormented by its current failure to stop the sandos. After many long hours bent over a laptop in their Tucson workshop, he made a curious discovery:

"Hey, Holly — I did some math. When two same-size number sequences cross each other, there are always gaps, numbers that never occur in pairs."

Chow gave this revelation some thought and made a suggestion:

"Then we use two sources for testing our ray gun — sweep one at the same rate all the time, and vary the timing on the other one on each sweep. That should cover all the possibilities."

"We hope," said Holzgraf doubtfully.

Chow was imagining the possibility of interstellar warfare.

"Yes we do."

Holzgraf readied a pair of powerful work lights over the Darlington Energetix starbot pen, turned them on, and adjusted their color temperature to a yellow-orange tint. He knew from past experience that starbot photosynthesis responded best to warm light.

"All set?"

Chow handed him a microwave generator enclosed in a long tube.

"You do the steady downsweep, and I'll vary the upsweep."

"Okay — if we get a hit, we stop immediately."

"Don't worry, we've got video, and we're logging the progression on my laptop."

Holzgraf then released the crab-like starbot Captain Donaldson captured into the pen. The thing sat there for a few minutes. Then it generated a pair of leaf-like fronds. After another few minutes, it began to scuttle around the edge, looking for a way out.

"Here we go, babe . . ."

Holzgraf pressed a button on his microwave apparatus. A small computer attached to the power supply dutifully swept the electromagnetic frequencies down and down through the entire microwave spectrum. He aimed it at the little starbot.

Chow flipped a switch on her own microwave generator and did the same. She had programmed the computer attached to her power supply to change the upsweep rate on each pass.

The workshop resounded with a warbling whine as the two microwave generators loudly interacted.

"Sweep one," called out Chow.

The robot was unaffected.

"Sweep two," she noted.

The robot continued probing the acrylic walls of the pen.

"Sweep three . . ."

The robot's forward legs blossomed into gecko-style footpads. It glued itself to one of the plastic panels and started climbing.

"Sweep four . . ."

Holzgraf lifted a leg over the top of the pen and kicked the silvery thing back down to the floor.

"Nice move, hon," grinned Chow. "Sweep five . . ."

Suddenly the little robot stopped in its tracks. It shuddered and dissolved into a pile of glittering sand.

"Holy crap!" shouted Holzgraf.

"Woo-hoo, we did it!" burbled Chow.

"Check the log — if you're idea of encryption is correct, we've got the new code, and we won't need sweeps at all."

37

SARZEAU arrived back in the states just in time to be late for a NITCOM meeting.

Congreve and company were eating pizza served from a food cart in the spectator area a quarter mile behind the wrecking yard perimeter. Between bites they marveled at the loot from Africa, particularly in the form of the defunct alien robot.

"This thing — Rudolph — red nose and all — it can talk?"

"Could talk. It died."

"Did it say anything about our visitors?"

"Not a word, I'm afraid. It's way older than they are."

This disappointing news led the group into a speculative debate over the best way to obliterate the starbots while humans still held an advantage.

"Why tell us about our DNA? So what if we're GMOs, like half our food? What's the point? The starbot motive?"

"Common ancestor crap . . . think they're sentimental? Or was it a ploy? Lull us to sleep while they plan our destruction?"

"They built an aircraft that can circle the world. What if they build an aerial armada? What if they're secretly hatching robo-rangers, combat ready?"

"Biding their time . . ."

"That's right. We've got a microwaver that works now, thanks to Holly and Guy. Strike first, I say."

Sarzeau was shocked by the warlike discussion. "Who says?"

General Upshaw looked up and took notice of the late arrival. "I do."

"Hang on, there. No one is going to start a war until I get my family out of harm's way."

General Congreve spread his arms. "Sorry, Marianne, but we can't subject national security to the whims of any individual."

Upshaw tried for conciliation. "Remember, our wave guns don't kill humans. Don't worry, we'll get your family out."

"Don't fucking kid me, Mo."

Wyatt held up a hand. "Relax, Sarzeau. The President is considering our plan of attack. He has not issued the *go code.*"

Sarzeau's eyes widened in anger and disbelief. She was about to erupt in vitriolic scorn, but then, with considerable difficulty, she managed to master her mood.

"All right. Here's my vote for presidential restraint."

General Congreve expelled a sigh of relief. "Don't be too hard on us. We are mindful of human cost, here, and across the world."

Sarzeau gestured toward the alien robot, lying on the command post's briefing table like a puppet with its strings cut. "That guy we unearthed — Rudy-Red-Nose — is a lot smarter than any starbot, or us, or our supercomputers. Roman taught him passable English in twenty-four hours. Get him a new battery, and maybe he'll tell you what the starbots are up to. You won't have to fire a shot."

General Weaver chuckled. "You're talking major surgery without anesthetic."

"Whatever."

Sarzeau waved and stalked out of the command center.

Holzgraf and Chow watched her go, exchanging glances with eyebrows raised.

▼

Sarzeau retreated to a far corner of the NITCOM operation, where she found an empty bivouac trailer, and let herself in. There she sat, contemplating her next move, waiting for nightfall and the cover of darkness.

While she was biding her time, Brom-Kat-Su floated out to the wrecking yard fence, calling for a parlay. General Weaver was delegated to represent NITCOM's interests.

"We demand the entity you have found. It belongs to us. It is" — the starbot chieftain hesitated, looking for the right word — "family," he finally decided.

"What entity is that? We have found quite a few things. Artifacts from before your time," said Weaver, being as evasive as possible.

"You cannot fool us. We see the signals. The entity is functional. And it is a small thing, of no value to humans."

Weaver made a phone call to the brain trust. He relayed the starbot demand and listened for guidance. After a short and cryptic conversation he ended the call.

"The entity — an ancient robot, if you will — is ours by right of salvage. We will keep it."

Brom's built-in loudspeaker crackled angrily. "At your peril, thief. But beware, justice must prevail." He turned back to the Quonset hut without another word. Weaver shivered involuntarily.

▼

Sarzeau discovered a grimy mirror on a wall in her trailer. She stood before it, with her stoney amulet in one hand and her little acorn in the other, and used them to summon her contact from . . . well, from where? No mailing address, she reminded herself.

"Whiskeyjack, talk to me!"

The mirror seemed to darken. A smoky form appeared.

Marianne.

"Where's my family, you bastard?"

I have set them on a course for humanity.

"Oh sure. You got them into trouble, now get them out!"

Consider well: that task belongs to those who guide Earth's fate.

"I thought you were on our side! But I guess, as a demon, why would you be?"

Whiskeyjack did not deign to reply. His smoky form faded

away, leaving Sarzeau to stare bitterly at her own troubled face. "Useless beast!"

Two hours and two trips to the portable toilets later, She was ready for action.

Gabriel? Can you hear me?

Hi, Mom. Where are you?

Not far. How about you two?

Dad says, underground. Door on the side. Concrete steps, big rooms dug out of the ground.

I will find you.

The spring evening was cool, and she stepped out toting a flak jacket she had found in the trailer. The Moon was down, and lights around the perimeter of the wrecking yard were bright, as attractive to Sarzeau as to the moths gyrating around each one.

Being careful to stroll in a lackadaisical manner, seemingly without purpose, she angled obliquely toward the wrecking yard perimeter fence. There she paused to murmur an invisibility spell with the classical rhymed couplets of practicing adepts:

> *Those who pass me shall not see*
> *None shall know where I may be*
> *About their business all shall tread*
> *With urgent errands in each head*

Of course she wouldn't actually be invisible, that she knew. She was just hoping to be ignored. Even that wasn't certain, because her book of occult lore was on a shelf back in Applefield, California, and her spell was entirely improvised from half-remembered verses.

Yet it seemed to work. She stood beside a beat-up Volkswagen Beetle just outside the fence while one of Congreve's patrols passed by. The soldiers didn't notice the woman standing there, off limits. They didn't even look in her direction. "How about that," she mused and started for the fence.

But three steps away she was accosted by Holzgraf and Chow, whose presence belied the force of her spell. She gasped. Her heart thumped.

"Whoa, you scared the shit out of me."

"Sorry," said Chow.

"How did you find me? I'm not looking for company."

"We followed you. We know what you're up to," said Holzgraf.

"What do you know? I'm out for a walk, that's all."

Chow giggled. Holzgraf shook his head.

"We thought you'd say that. We have something for you."

Chow lifted a compact version of their microwave gun into view. "This is a prototype, so be careful with it."

Sarzeau took the device into her own hands.

"How do you know it works?"

"We tested. Works on the bots."

Sarzeau hefted the gun experimentally.

"What about human dupes — the sandos?"

"Not sure."

"Mmm."

"You'll get five, maybe six or seven shots, before our pathetic battery dies, so pick your targets."

Holzgraf patted Sarzeau on the shoulder. Chow gave her a quick hug.

"Stay safe, girl."

The pair faded away into the night, and Sarzeau turned to the problem of the fence.

She waited for another patrol to pass by, then opened the flak jacket she was carrying and carefully positioned it over the razor wire. Using it to protect herself from serious wounds, she clambered up, over, and down into the wrecking yard proper.

▼

She was fifty yards from the Stone Valley Scrap & Salvage head-quarters and its rusty Quonset hut. A vast accumulation of wrecked automobiles, trucks, and earthmoving equipment stood between her and her goal, but lanes between the vehicles looked passable, and nothing was moving through them.

Gabriel?

Her mental probe, usually effective with her precocious son, received no response. She took a deep breath, got a good grip on her microwave gun, and eased herself into the sheet metal jungle.

Just past a Ford Ranger pickup that had suffered a rollover, she was threatened by one of the little crab-like starbots that was busy gathering junk. It dropped the wires in its claws and attached itself to her left leg.

"Ahhh!"

She tilted her gun downward, and pressed the trigger.

Whooosh

The starbot exploded into sandy particles.

"Hah! Take that, you damn rat!"

With eyes wide and a big dose of adrenaline pulsing through her veins, she cautiously advanced twenty yards before she sensed another obstacle. Negligent footfalls, scraping noises, and the creaky slam of a door brought her to a halt behind a forlorn Lexus sedan. She crouched down.

"Urrrrrhhh . . ."

What was that? She poked her head up over the hood of the Lexus to find out, and there was a figure standing on the other side of the car, staring at her.

"Oh shit! Jesus Christ!"

"Urrrrrhhh . . ."

Sarzeau sucked in her breath, told herself to stay calm.

"Who? Who are you?"

"Urrrrrhhh . . ."

The figure looked like a man, possibly Hispanic. It was wearing bib overalls over a Phoenix Cardinals T-shirt. It had a floppy felt hat on its head, but it wasn't really a person anymore, Sarzeau was sure of that.

"Sando!" she exclaimed. *Zombie* is what she thought. "Um, you work here? I'm Marianne, nice to meet you . . ."

The figure raised a hand with a silvery weapon gripped in its fingers that resembled the little Beretta she often carried as a backup piece.

Bap

Sarzeau dropped to the ground just as the figure aimed and fired. She heard a pellet explode off the wreck behind her. Pretty soon she could also hear shuffling footsteps, moving around the Lexus, coming for her. She groped for the trigger of her wave gun, put a finger on it. Now the sando was only a few feet away. She rolled back on her butt, tilted the weapon in her attacker's general direction and pressed the trigger.

Whirrr

The beam of microwaves was invisible, but the sound told her the weapon was firing.

The menacing figure raised its own handgun, aimed it at Sarzeau, but stopped moving before it could fire another pellet. Within a couple of seconds it was shaking all over.

"Urrrrrhhh . . ."

Sparkling particles flew every which way. Then the figure dissolved into a pile of sand, leaving its clothes in a heap on the desert floor.

Sarzeau herself was shaking all over. She picked up the figure's gun and gave it a close inspection. Even as she was examining the details, it too dissolved. She clapped her hands to throw off the powdery residue. Then she reached for the sando's hat, shook out the dust, and mashed it down over her own head. A thin disguise, but it made her feel brave.

Soon she was approaching the Quonset hut's wide-open entrance. Light was pouring out into the yard, and she was careful to peek inside with just one eye. The only activity she could see was happening at the far end of the cavernous interior, where three ex-human sandos were working on some unidentifiable machinery.

Just inside the entrance, to the left, she spotted a rectangular pit and what looked like a concrete stairwell descending into a dark cellar. She was about to risk a dash to the stairs when she spotted smaller door on her right, half-closed. Which way to go?

Gabe, honey. You down there?

She waited impatiently for a response. She was contemplating ugly possibilities and steeling herself for the worst when a familiar mental tickle touched her mind.

Yeah, Mom. I was asleep.

Well, wake up, kiddo. Is Dad with you?

Right here. Dad says, use the side door. Down the stairs, turn left.

Sarzeau sidestepped to the door and peeked inside. The large open bay where human duplicates were tending starbot machinery came into view. A few feet along the wall stood a tall gate bristling with peculiar devices, some of them obviously electronic. Was that the security gate referred to by the famous tour members? Hard to know. Beyond the gate she could see the rectangular pit and an alternate set of concrete stairs.

She waited until she was pretty certain the sandos weren't paying attention, then quickly dodged past the gate and hurried down the stairs.

She found herself in the original wrecking yard cellar, a concrete room where large casks stored recovered motor oil, and where bins held piles of usable tires and stacks of auto glass.

To her left was a ragged hole in the concrete. Beyond it she could see a passageway, also concrete, but irregularly shaped, as if poured from a rapidly oscillating nozzle. The product of some starbot machine, no doubt.

She turned into the passage and moved along it with her microwaver at the ready, just in case she ran into another bot or sando.

After a dozen cautious steps the passage opened into a wider area. Here the walls were articulated with narrow horizontal layers. She thought the room looked like the interior of one of those 3D-printed houses she had seen in online photos.

Three doorways opened out of the room. She pondered her Monty Hall problem, a real life version of the old *Let's Make a Deal* show on TV: she had a two-thirds probability of picking the wrong exit, and that meant a two-thirds probability of running into serious opposition.

While she was trying to decide, a miniature starbot scuttled over and attempted to climb onto her foot. She gave it a good kick and launched the thing across the room, where it landed on its back. She watched it flip itself over, climb the nearest wall, and timidly latch onto what might be a small recharging station.

Gabe? Your mom is lost. Little help, please.

I hear you. Dad says go straight, we're two doors down.

Sarzeau moved forward into another irregularly formed passage. At the second doorway she turned to her left. A figure inside sprang out of hiding and pulled her into a tight embrace.

"Ahhh!" she squeaked, terrified that a sando had caught her.

"Hey, babe, it's me! Tom! Your loving husband." He quickly backed away and gestured toward his body. "Except no showers here. I don't smell so good."

Sarzeau clapped a hand to her face.

"Jesus Christ, I'm jumpy enough — don't scare me like that!"

Gabriel came forward and gently put his arms around Sarzeau, tucked his head into her waist.

"Thanks for coming, Mom. How do you like Dad's beard?"

Sarzeau brushed a hand over Wagstaff's face, checking the stubble.

"How long have you been stuck down here?"

"Two weeks? I think that's it. Hard to count the days without daylight."

She looked at her family. She was expecting emaciated bodies, something horrifying like the inmates of a Nazi concentration camp, but husband and son looked healthy.

"What are they feeding you?"

Wagstaff chuckled. "Mushrooms. Either they grow them or make them, not sure which."

"Ugh."

"And water to drink." He pointed into the passageway. "They don't metabolize like we do, so we made a latrine down the hall there."

"Wonderful. Let's get you guys the hell out of here."

Wagstaff angled his head uncertainly and gestured toward Sarzeau's microwaver.

"Don't you think you ought to use that gun first? What if Gabe and I aren't who you think we are?"

Sarzeau bit her lip. She scowled. She raised the weapon, aimed it, positioned her finger on the trigger . . . then tilted it back down to her side.

"I can't do it. Maybe you're a couple of sandos in training. I don't care — you're my family, bots or not."

38

WAIT, WAIT, I want to show you something." Wagstaff fell back behind Sarzeau, who was hustling her family toward the stairway and the Quonset hut exit.

"Come on, Tom, pretty soon the bots are going to figure out they've lost a hostage. They won't be happy."

"No, you've got to see it. Over here . . ."

He pulled at her sleeve and led her toward a side door that opened onto a wide underground bay, a veritable factory.

"Look, see that — ?" he whispered.

"See what?" Work lights, apparently some form of LEDs, bathed the factory floor in a dim orange glow.

"That thing they're building. All those parts, funny shapes."

"Yeah, another one of their oddball machines."

Wagstaff pointed at the activity and then at the ceiling and the sky above. "It's not just a machine. It's a ship."

"How do you know that?" Sarzeau was also whispering, and her rasp was getting louder and harsher, reflecting her urge to hurry an escape.

"A scary man said so, Mom," muttered Gabriel.

"Scary man?"

"Yeah," confirmed Wagstaff. "The original sando himself, old Lockbot Lockwood."

"Why would he say that? No one else has heard a word about their plans."

"Pride? An attempt to show us what their intentions are? An effort to prevent all-out war?"

"Okay, I'll bite. Not a takeover? Then what? What did Ambassador Lockwood disclose to you, the fearless reporter?"

"Ouch. Mock if you want, but we did some investigating on our own, and I have the skinny."

"And . . ."

"They really are building a ship. Getting ready to head out into deep space."

"News flash, the starbots already do that."

"They do, but very slowly. It took them a hundred years to establish their base in this godforsaken wrecking yard."

He pointed at an unfinished section of what might be a ship under construction.

"See the cradle molded into the middle there? The huge bolts?"

"Yeah . . ."

"That's gotta be the engine room. Only it's empty. They don't actually *have* an engine. I think that's why they're here. They're looking for one."

"Well, they came to the wrong planet. We're all out."

"Yeah, but I'm betting they think their creators left one lying around. We know those creatures got here, long before the starbots. Evidence is in our DNA, right?"

Sarzeau sagged against the doorway. She turned to Gabriel.

"What does Whiskeyjack say?"

"He said I made a good infiltration."

"That's all?"

"What's an infiltration?"

Sarzeau let out an impatient sigh. "So, starbot factory. Hidden under the wrecking yard. Missing part."

"Not a highlight of the famous Tour," noted Wagstaff.

"Maybe Whiskeyjack was onto them," mused Sarzeau, "knew we had to get inside on our own, knew we'd find something when we got here."

She pulled her smartphone from a side pocket, aimed it into the starbot factory, and clicked off several photos.

"Come on, we need to talk to the brain trust They have no idea."

They started for the stairs, but as they reached the room's exit, the once-human James Lockwood appeared to block their way.

"You. Think to betray our trust. But you cannot. Cannot leave."

His voice, which seemed to come directly from his chest, was loud and monotonic. It reverberated around the hard concrete walls.

Sarzeau almost fainted. Surely half a dozen sandos and bots heard the stern command. Soon they would come running.

"Captain Lockwood, yes? I'm Marianne Sarzeau. We met a few years ago, down in Tucson. Remember?"

"You cannot leave. War will follow."

"I promise that won't happen. I have a lot of clout, a lot of influence . . ."

"You cannot leave."

Evidently Lockwood, in his current incarnation, wasn't quite as personable as formerly. Sarzeau took note.

"The starbots can recreate you whenever they need to, am I right? You know, if something bad should happen?"

Lockwood seemed puzzled by the question.

"That is true. We have many powers."

"Thought so."

Sarzeau brought up her microwave gun and pressed the trigger.

"Microwaves? Oh, please . . ."

Lockwood smirked at what he thought was a useless weapon. But his contempt turned to horror as he started vibrating, went into robotic convulsions, and promptly dissolved into glistening particles of sand that sprinkled themselves all over the concrete floor.

39

SARZEAU, Tom Wagstaff, and little Gabriel were gathered in the NITCOM command post, on trial for their unauthorized penetration of the starbot base. They were facing a skeptical jury, and Wagstaff thought it best to begin their account with the headlines.

"That Quonset hut is just the tip of an iceberg. The starbots have carved an underground factory out of the desert right beneath our feet."

"You saw this?"

"Look at my wife's photos, you'll see it too."

Walter Melrose, the new acting Secretary of State, joined the NITCOM brain trust via Skype from his office in Washington. "Show me," he said.

Sarzeau held up her phone, pointed it at the large computer display that dominated one wall, and ran through her photos for him.

"They're doing something down there, I guess," opined Melrose. "Hard to tell what, though," The secretary was unwilling to concede anything to people he regarded as out-of-control renegades.

"They are in the process of building a ship, a big one," insisted Wagstaff.

Barney Wyatt was confused. "They already built one, that's how they got to Zimbabwe, and now China."

"This one is different. It's interstellar."

"How would you know that?"

"It wasn't on the Tour. Lockwood told us."

"Lockwood told you? And you believe him?" marveled Wyatt.

"They want us to know that world conquest is not on their agenda."

"Oh, so now you're a foreign policy expert?"

Wagstaff was insulted by the evident disbelief and the hostile questions.

"Look, Mr. — um, I don't think we've met. You are?"

"National Security Advisor to the President," said Wyatt.

"Aha. I think the President will want his advisors to bring him our intelligence findings, don't you? What we found out while we scarfed down all those mushrooms."

Wyatt sat back in his chair. "Of course."

"So here they are. We've all been wondering why the starbots showed up. The big mystery. Well, Gabe and I found out. The ship we're talking about? I didn't see any sign of an engine. I think they're looking for whatever their creators brought to our planet, way back when they showed up here."

"An engine. What do you think propelled the ship they've already built?"

Astronomer Nancy Weatherall, away in China, was listening to the discussion via satellite phone. She was intrigued by Wagstaff's guesses.

"If the starbots had a faster-than-light deal, they wouldn't need all those bushes they sent," she asserted. "Took forever. They wouldn't need to manufacture themselves right here on Earth, either. They would have ridden here in style. We know the starbots are looking everywhere for their biological forebears. Maybe those creatures did have such an engine, and the bots want it."

"So they're building a ship. What's the power source to run that factory you spotted?"

"Think. You already know," said Wagstaff. "The brownouts in all the local towns around here. The Palo Verde nuclear plant is next door, and they tap into the power it produces. Probably why they set up shop here."

"That's absurd. How is that possible?"

"You got me. Lockwood wouldn't discuss it."

General Upshaw tapped a finger against his head. "Forgive us for drilling you people. You make it sound as though Lockwood, my former assistant and now sando *numero uno,* was your host instead of your prison guard. That makes me suspicious. How do we know your fantastic tale isn't disinformation designed to conceal their real intentions?"

Sarzeau was tapping a foot, barely able to contain her sense of outrage. She folded her arms.

"We don't know. We can't be sure. But, tell me this — why do you think they're tearing up Africa? Tearing up China? They're on the hunt, and I think we should be too."

Congreve raised his hands to signal a timeout.

"Okay, let us think. I should throw the three of you in the stockade for violating our operational protocols. But I'm not going to do that. Instead, you're pardoned for actions above and beyond, how's that?"

"Beats jail," growled Wagstaff.

"On the other hand, I wonder about you, how things went in custody. Guy?"

Sarzeau was still holding the microwave gun Chow handed her on the way into the starbot base. Holzgraf held out his hand to take it. The color drained from Sarzeau's face. She shrank back in horror.

"Noooo . . ."

Chow reached around and snatched the weapon away.

"Let's find out who our spies really are," said Congreve. "Fire at will."

Holzgraf took the waver and aimed it at the brave explorers. Sarzeau dodged in front of her son and husband, making herself into a clumsy shield.

"Don't you dare!" she shouted.

Holzgraf pressed the trigger.

Zooowww

The gun sang softly as its invisible beam painted the trio with microwaves in two different well-chosen frequencies.

After thirty seconds Holzgraf put down the gun.

"Hey, everybody . . ."

The sustained blast had no effect. Wagstaff, Gabriel, and Sarzeau were shown to be authentic human beings.

"Oh my God!" sighed Sarzeau. Her knees wobbled. She started to collapse. Wagstaff gently deposited her into the command post's only comfortable chair.

General Weaver, her occasional supervisor, squeezed her shoulder. "It's okay. You and your family, that's who we hoped you were."

Phase **5**

40

SOMETHING to show you, sir."

The alert soldier in charge of NITCOM's surveillance cameras was back in the command post outside the Stone Valley Scrap & Salvage wrecking yard with another disquieting video on his laptop.

General Congreve gestured to a media table where various wires and plugs were sprouting.

"Let's send it to the big screen."

As the video clip rolled, a section of the Quonset hut roof slid open.

"Uh-oh, we've seen this movie."

Suddenly a blurry object flew out of the opening and disappeared out of frame.

"Now, be damned — those bots are hauling chili."

The soldier replayed the clip and paused over the blurry streak.

"We don't have a clean image — I guess they don't want us to get one — but this is a much smaller object than the other ship we've seen."

"What's it doing?"

"Can't be sure, sir. Not a mind reader."

Congreve was pondering the matter when his phone rang; NORAD calling.

"Got an update on starbot traffic, General. Thought you'd like to know."

"If it means you can spot an alien vehicle for me, I sure do."

The caller chuckled. "That's why I'm on the horn before you call to rank me out — good news for a change. We are tracking an unidentified object in low polar orbit, and it ain't Saint Nick."

"Details . . ?"

"Speed is barely fast enough to remain in orbit, and it requires a power boost now and then to stay aloft."

"It's got thrusters?"

"I don't know about that. It gets a pretty good jolt whenever it passes over industrial scale power plants."

Congreve put a hand over the phone mouthpiece and signaled urgently to the surveillance operator.

"Check the latest brownouts for me, Sergeant. Toot sweet."

"Yes sir."

Congreve resumed his phone call with a query. "You said polar orbit? Meaning it passes over everything?"

"As the Earth turns underneath, after several orbits, that's affirm."

"How do you account for that trajectory?"

"We don't."

"Take a guess."

"Well, if this thing was Russian, I'd say it's a reconnaissance mission. They appear to be doing a survey, looking for something."

"Thank you, son. Keep us informed."

The surveillance specialist ended his own local phone call.

"Brownouts in Tonopah and Buckeye at ninety minute intervals since that thing launched, sir."

"How many?"

"Three, sir."

"How long since you recorded the launch?"

"Around eight hours, give or take."

Congreve rallied his team to spread the news. The brain trust reacted with nods and shrugs."

"Who's in China, Vern? Mo?"

General Weaver consulted a smartphone app. "Looks like Marianne's dad, Major Ray Bagwell, and a U.S. army detachment. Plus the Chinese, of course."

"And what have they got?"

"Not sure."

Congreve was soon on the phone to China, where the FULTAP contingent was observing operations in Xi'an.

"What's going on in the Middle Kingdom, Major?"

Pause.

"No joy? Are the bots still on scene?"

Pause.

"Any idea where they went?"

Pause.

Sarzeau was studying a pile of photo prints from Great Zimbabwe. Her gaze fastened on the image of a starbot precursor. She had been unable to decide whether it looked Chinese or Mexican, and like the rest of the team, she had been leaning toward China, well populated since antiquity. But now, overhearing one side of Congreve's call, doubts were growing.

"Is that Major Bagwell? Let me talk to him."

"Hold on, here's your witch."

Congreve passed the phone to Sarzeau.

"Ray? Oh, Dad — it's you. How are you? Find anything out there?"

Sergeant Major Sarzo, Sarzeau's father, was resigned to a failed mission. "The starbots are gone. They dug a big hole near the pyramid, smashed an awful lot of those terracotta soldiers, and duplicated a whole company of Chinese forces. Then they got back in their ship and took off. The sandos all collapsed, and we just found a lot of bodies — the soldiers they replaced — down in the pit. Ugly stuff."

"But no evidence of the biological aliens, the old ones, is that right?"

"We're still looking. Your pals Garibaldi and Pomeroy are hopeful."

"What do you think?"

"The astronomer with us, Dr. Weatherall — she thinks we've drawn a blank. I'm inclined to agree, but we haven't turned all the stones over yet."

"Take care, Dad," said Sarzeau. She handed the phone back to Congreve.

"Whatever the bots are looking for — engine, tombs, who knows — they didn't find it in China. That explains the satellite they launched."

41

GENERAL CONGREVE and Barney Wyatt were studying a detailed map of Egypt.

"Lots of possibilities there. Giza, Aswan, Valley of the Kings. We better be prepared for heat and thirst."

"Throw in an unfriendly government, and a hostile population. Going to be tough."

"Why Egypt? Why not Cambodia? It's the next stop after China."

"If the bots were interested in Cambodia, they'd be there already. They're not."

Congreve nodded. "I talked to Wally's deputy. State Department has a call in to the Egyptian government, making the usual requests for our assistance."

Sarzeau was still looking at Nikki Traeger's photos from Great Zimbabwe.

"Like everyone, I was leaning toward China," she mused. "But the more I look, the more I think *Mexico.*"

She handed a photo print of the starbot precursor mural to General Upshaw, who put on his reading glasses for a close examination.

"I'm no art historian."

He handed the picture to Congreve, who gave it a quick look.

"No human lived in the New World when the biological aliens were here. Seems like a long shot," said he.

Sarzeau was not easily dissuaded. "No? Remember — no modern human lived *anywhere on Earth* when those spooky old joes arrived."

"I say, Egypt," said Congreve, overriding her objections. "What about it? Show of hands?"

Upshaw raised his hand. "Egypt."

Wyatt did likewise. "Yeah, that's what I think."

Weaver joined in. "Egypt. I'm betting on Valley of the Kings. Anyone want to take my bet?"

Congreve nodded. "Well, then, Egypt it is."

"I'll bake the order to FULTAP," said Upshaw. "Let's marshal the troops in Cairo, with instructions to move out on short notice."

Sarzeau snorted. "You guys! You don't really know where the bots are going. And, hey — they don't know either. That's why they've got that spacecraft cruising around up there. We should bring it down before they get the jump on us all over again."

"Good idea," agreed Wyatt. He stroked his chin. "We could shut down the nuclear plant, that would do the job."

Congreve rolled his eyes. "Black out Phoenix? Kill power that two million people depend on? Come on, Barney, no one's ready for that."

Holly Chow had another idea.

"Let's talk to Nancy. That satellite will be passing over one of our deep space networks pretty soon. Can those big antennas transmit our microwave code? Maybe we can dissolve the thing."

▼

Weatherall was waiting in Xi'an for a flight to Japan and then home when Upshaw reached her via satellite phone. She listened to his proposal and reacted with grudging appreciation.

"Where is the botcraft right now?"

"Over the Aleutian islands, heading south."

"We'll need one of NASA's 70 meter antennas. Our best — make that only — chance is Canberra, in Australia. DSS 43 is the big boy down there. Does it have the wattage to bring down a satellite? I know a couple of the admin guys. I'll make a call on ITF authority, but get Holly or Guy to send out their code."

"We'll get on it."

"And make them use really strong encryption. That code is how we're going to beat those bots."

"Understood. You take care. See you at the wrecking yard."

Holly and Guy thought about encryption and decided that the starbots should not be underestimated. Holly used a Sharpie to write the pair of code frequency numbers in reverse order on paper, and Guy sent the message off via fax. The analog texting system that once held sway in the not-quite-modern world was so obsolete, everyone figured they were safe.

A follow-up call to DSN Canberra completed their preparations. Now it was just a matter of waiting for the starbot satellite to reach Australia.

Twenty minutes went by. Members of the NITCOM brain trust were colliding with each other as they paced back and forth in the command post, awaiting news, good or bad.

A hundred miles in the sky, the starbot satellite passed high above DSN Canberra and continued onward over the Southern Ocean.

A few minutes later the phone rang with NORAD on the line.

"We do not see your rogue satellite. We did pick up a blizzard of small particles in that orbit. Could be re-entry debris."

"Oh yes it could!" trumpeted Congreve.

The rest of the team performed high fives, fist bumps, and elbow tags.

Sarzeau positioned herself near the door. "I need a flight to Mexico."

Weaver wasn't persuaded. "Fools errand, Broomer."

"Maybe so, Vern, but we need to act while we've got an advantage. Put me on a plane and let me prove you wrong."

42

NICOLETTE TRAEGER, the enterprising journalist, was lounging in a fancy café on a roofed-over patio seven floors above the Zócalo plaza in the heart of old Mexico City, nursing a margarita. Blended, no salt.

She had been in the country for a week, working her phone and her feet hard, hoping to score another interstellar scoop. But her inquiries had yet to unlock the secret she suspected was buried under some pre-Columbian ruin somewhere out in the Mexican countryside.

She was waiting for her only reliable Mexican connection, a fellow journalist she had met while covering the civil strife in Nicaragua as an eager rookie reporter, many years ago.

Soon after her second margarita appeared, so did her contact, Nazario Peña, a thin and handsome man of fifty years or so.

"Naz! Finally, here you are!"

She reached out a hand in greeting. Peña kissed it with a flourish and took a seat.

"My dear woman, it's been years, and you look better than ever. What brings you to Mexico?"

"You, Naz."

He raised an eyebrow.

"Not really, I suppose . . ."

Peña made a long face, pretending to be saddened by the slight.

"Instead . . . I have reason to believe we might find a key to the starbot visitation here. I'm investigating."

Peña laughed. "I saw your act on TV — aliens fixing our DNA! You are a star."

"But not a bot, thank you very much. Look at this . . ."

She showed him a photo of the Zimbabwe mural depicting one of the starbot precursors.

"What do you think? Look Chinese?"

"Hmm."

"Or more like Mexican? That's what I think, why I'm here. You see the resemblance? Aztec? Maya? Zapotec?"

Peña slowly shook his head. "I couldn't tell if it was Eskimo, Nikki."

"Okay, what about dig sites? Rumors of big finds? Strange finds? Anything?"

Peña caught a waiter striding by and ordered a Negra Modelo.

"There was a proposal to dig up a street about three blocks over, other side of the park," he said, squeezing a lime into his beer. "You know, that's where they found the famous Sun Stone."

"Yeah?"

"And the proposal was denied. Somebody with a building in the way paid somebody, no doubt. Anyway, there's a guy you should meet, he was pounding the drum for the excavation."

"Sounds promising. Who is he?"

"Professor of art history at the university. I interviewed him for *La Prensa* . . . I'll call, set it up."

Three hours after Sarzeau landed at Mexico City's international airport on an Aeromexico flight from Phoenix, Roman Garibaldi joined her on the last leg of his homeward journey from China, via Hawaii, on United Air Lines.

He brought with him the name of an expert on Mexican archeological work, an art professor teaching at The National Autonomous University, someone named Inigo Garcia.

"Who gave you this?"

"General Weaver called some company called American TV & Appliance. They seem to know everything."

"Spook Central, Roman."

Five blocks northwest of the Zócalo they entered an elaborately carved wooden door on a narrow street and found themselves in a wide courtyard arcade, two stories high, bristling with columns and milling students. They noticed a map glowing on an electronic billboard under one of the archways and headed over to learn Professor Garcia's office location.

A cluster of students crowding around the map gave way at their approach, revealing a forty-ish woman in khaki shorts and a photographer's vest studying the university's layout.

"Well hello, it's the famous journalist," exclaimed Garibaldi.

Nikki Traeger nearly jumped out of her skin.

"Ohhh *shit!*"

Sarzeau lurched backward, stunned to silence by the unexpected encounter.

Garibaldi, however, had watched the journalist operate just long enough to be amused by her initiative. "Looking for Inigo Garcia?" he guessed.

Traeger giggled. "Guilty! How did you know?"

"We have an appointment. Join us?"

The reporter swallowed and nodded sheepishly.

Sarzeau pointed to the sheaf of photo prints Traeger was holding. "Bring your photos," she croaked. "That's what we're doing."

▼

Professor Doctor Inigo Garcia was a portly old man with a wild halo of white hair. A fringe of white beard outlined a peevishly downturned mouth. He declined to speak English to his American visitors, but luckily, Traeger was fluent in Spanish.

"You see the sour expression, right?" she noted quizzically. "He wonders why he, a Mexican academic, might know anything of value to us Americans and our jet airplanes."

Sarzeau caught the hostile drift and thought how best to step through the swamp of resentment. "Sir, we are ignorant of Mexico and its archeological history, but eager to learn. Ms. Traeger made some very interesting photographs of a mural we located in an African dig site. We're here from our government to get your professional opinion of them."

Garcia donned reading glasses, gathered the pictures from Garibaldi and Traeger, and slowly leafed through them, mumbling quietly over each one.

"He says the mural is a remarkable find," reported Traeger. "He wants to know who made it."

"That's a No Fly Zone," said Garibaldi.

Garcia pointed to one of the images.

"He thinks this figure is significant, but he can't ID the style without knowing more. Shouldn't we explain the origin?" wondered Traeger. "Might help break the ice."

Garibaldi was about to reject the idea when Sarzeau raised a hand to shut him up.

"Tell him it's from the starbot ancestors," she said. "Make him feel like he's in on a big secret."

Garcia nodded. He smiled, having already guessed the truth. He waved a close-up photo of the alien figure at his visitors, snapped a finger against it, let loose a paragraph of Spanish. Traeger nodded.

"He thinks this figure shows hints of Chinese characteristics. He wants us to go to China."

"Been there, done that, got the T-shirt," grouched Garibaldi.

"He agrees that some see a resemblance between Chinese and Mexican art, but the idea is controversial, and he isn't sure which human culture this might have influenced. Maybe both."

"But not Egyptian, right?" said Sarzeau. "Ask him that."

Garcia shook his head. He laughed out loud.

"Imbéciles! Nunca en la vida!"

He handed the photo prints back, all except one.

"His professional opinion — the imagery is remarkable, and he wants a souvenir."

"Sure, we don't mind."

"Ask him about dig sites, any place stuff like this might have turned up."

Garcia spoke at length, shrugged, and leaned forward across his work table to shake his visitors' hands.

"He hopes we find answers to our questions, and maybe Catalina can answer them."

"Catalina?"

Traeger repeated the question.

"Um, it's Catalina Delgado. She's staff archeologist at the National Museum of Anthropology."

"Never heard of it," moaned Garibaldi.

"And now he says, *adiós.*"

43

A TAXI drove the Americans four miles west of the university to the anthropology museum, a low ultra-modern building almost lost in the surprisingly dense urban forest of Tamayo Park.

Garibaldi was curious, but dubious. "What is this place?"

Traeger put a finger over her mouth. "Be polite, doc. It's a world famous collection of pre-Columbian treasures. Think Louvre, think Prado. Pride of Mexico."

An attendant at the reception counter drew a line on a paper map with a highlighter pen and pointed down the wide interior promenade.

"Delgado, *Allá abajo, Amigos . . .'*

At the end of the promenade a corridor branched off to the right. Traeger led the way along its length, reading names on the many offices. "Here we are . . ." she said, and pushed open a glass doorway.

They had arrived at an archeological laboratory where Catalina Delgado, a wiry woman of middle years, was bent over a sorting table littered with shards of stone. She looked up, rubbed her hands on her apron, and gestured toward her project.

"A Mayan jigsaw puzzle. What do you think it says?" she asked in good, lightly accented English.

Traeger stared blankly at the carved Mayan glyphs. "All hail the Jaguar King?"

Delgado chuckled musically. "Not a bad guess. Personally, I can't read it yet, all except this piece, 'jackal.'"

Sarzeau stared at the stony chunks, which seemed as strange to her as the starbots. Then she noticed that Garibaldi was hanging back at the door. He looked very uncomfortable.

"It's okay, Roman — there's no actual presence here. Just a history telegram."

Delgado aimed a Hasselblad camera at her work and snapped a documentary photo. Then she indicated a desk and chairs.

"Sit, sit. I heard from Inigo. He said I should shoo you away with false promises."

"Really . . ."

"Is he right? You are not to be trusted?" Delgado's eyes sparkled with curiosity, belying her coolly aloof words. "Show me the mural."

Traeger handed over her photo prints. Delgado sifted through them, stopping on the close-up of the alien ancestor.

"So . . ." murmured Delgado, "this is one of them, one of the visitors who inscribed our DNA, yes?"

"What we're wondering, Madame Doctor," began Garibaldi, "is whether this visual style might have influenced pre-Columbian Mexican art."

"Inigo mentioned the idea. He thinks it is absurd."

"And you?" asked Sarzeau. "Professor Garcia thinks *we're* absurd. What do you think?"

Delgado picked up a large magnifying glass and studied the alien close-up all over again.

"What I think is . . . the head, wide, angular, eyes set wide. A slight similarity tugs my thoughts. We sometimes see imagery like that in the form of paired snakes."

She tapped the photo print.

"But — I can't really offer an expert opinion. What I can do is show you some examples in our collection. Then you must judge."

▼

Delgado led her visitors into the museum's maze of exhibition halls, where they passed by a number of stunning pre-Columbian sculpture pieces mounted on pedestals and set among glass cases filled with superbly decorated pottery.

They turned a corner, and there was the famous Aztec Calendar Stone, brightly lit against its white backdrop. It dominated a room chock-a-block full of more statuary and artifacts, all carved in a visual vocabulary that puzzled and repelled the ignorant Americans.

Around another corner they saw a tall and bulky sculpture piece, surrounded by wide-eyed school kids on a field trip.

"Behold, *Coatlicue,*" announced Delgado. "Here you see the paired snake heads I mentioned."

What they were looking at was a stupendous figure of many disparate parts, almost ten feet tall, carved from a huge block of volcanic andesite rock. The statue's head was a cleverly designed pair of snake heads turned nose to nose. The resulting wide-set eyes and fangs radiated terrific power and menace. It looked like nothing Sarzeau, Garibaldi, and Traeger had ever seen — hideous, commanding, deeply unsettling — a visual catalog of grisly pre-Columbian religious ideas.

"Who?" asked Sarzeau. "Co-at-what?"

"CO-AT-LEE-QUAY," repeated Delgado. "The mother goddess of fertility and death."

"Are those *snakes* woven into her skirt?" wondered Garibaldi, balking at the idea.

"Oh yes, she is deadly. Her belt is a pair of snakes, cinched tight around skulls front and back, with their heads dangling as tassels. Notice her necklace — alternating human hearts and severed hands."

Garibaldi was wrestling with his own demons.

"I can't really look at her. I mean, notice how she's leaning forward, like she's coming to get us. Her hands and feet have tiger claws."

"Whew, nobody mess with the Snake Lady," said an awestruck Traeger.

Sarzeau was circumspect. "I've seen worse monsters."

Traeger laughed at the idea. "Impossible! Where? How?"

"Oh, in a dream, I guess you'd say. Two different ones, Ogg and Whiskeyjack. Ogg was evil, but Whiskeyjack is a good guy. Let's not judge old Serpent Skirt too harshly."

"Do you think," offered Delgado hesitantly, "that she resembles the creature in your mural?"

All three Americans nodded. "Yes, she does."

"You know, diggers have turned up other statues like this one, only not as big, not as well preserved." She shrugged fatalistically. "Some scholars take the position that the serpent skirt sculptures, plural, are *tzitzimime,* deities from the stars who only wait for the Sun to expire before they gobble us all up."

"You believe in that stuff?" asked Garibaldi suspiciously. The mere idea made him nervous.

"I'm a good catholic woman. I go to mass. This is art."

Sarzeau, a catholic herself, absorbed the distinction with respect. "When was this statue carved? Where?"

"We date it to around 1450," said Delgado. "It was found buried in the city's main square in 1790 while workmen were digging a canal. But it couldn't have been made there."

"I think the artist was channeling some residue of an alien presence," concluded Sarzeau. "That's what we noticed in Zimbabwe. And sure enough, we found a robot whose clock was still ticking after two hundred thousand years."

Delgado frowned. "What would aliens be doing in Mexico? There were no people here that long ago, none at all."

"No people anywhere, ma'am," said Garibaldi. "Just animals, a lot of them brutish, many dangerous."

He closed his eyes and forced himself to touch the fearsome statue's serpent skirt. His fingertips brushed the stone and he jerked them back as if the statue were hot as a stove. "Any digs going on here in Mexico with prospects for another Coatlicue discovery? Maybe near the studio where this one was made?"

Delgado sat down on the statue's pedestal, rested her elbows on her thighs, cupped her chin with her hands, and spent a moment lost in thought. Then:

"A man called Borel is digging up an old aqueduct on the road to Teotihuacan, about thirty kilometers east of here. It's a bit controversial. Borel is American, his dig is American — done with our cooperation, of course — but the money comes from *el Norte*. A possibility for you."

"Does he know what he's doing?" asked Traeger.

"He is dedicated, he is intelligent, he is accomplished . . . but he is also romantic. I don't know what he's after. I doubt he does either."

44

WHY HERE?" asked Sarzeau. She was standing in a stone-enclosed field bordering the Avenue of the Dead on the outskirts of Teotihuacan, the famously abandoned pre-Columbian metropolis a few miles northeast of Mexico City.

Aaron "Ari" Borel, Ph.D., A.I.A, S.A.A., a grizzled American archeologist in T-shirt and shorts, reached into a wooden box he was holding and held up a small chip of andesite rock to answer Sarzeau's question.

"Look and learn. This fragment shows a sharp break, a shear. Pretty sure it was struck off a much larger block. The work of a sculptor. Right here below our feet."

He dropped the shard into the box and picked up another small object. "See? Here's a bead. Personal decoration." He rummaged around and exhibited a tiny fleck of bright metal on a fingertip. "Gold filings? We got 'em."

He ducked into the shadows of a canvas canopy and returned with a long and sharp black stone. "Obsidian knife blade."

He clapped his hands to dust them off, rubbed his palms on his T-shirt, and adjusted his worn *Santa Fe* themed baseball cap.

Sarzeau was impressed, but skeptical. "Don't be offended, but you sound like an advertisement."

Borel grimaced. "Yeah, well, I've got sponsors who are bigger doubters than you three . . . Spofford and his penny-pinching foundation directors." He shrugged. "So I haven't hit paydirt yet — the signs are all here. This was a major habitation. Possibly a religious locus, or the studio of artisans, more likely. Who knows? Your favorite statue might have been carved right here."

"Coatlicue?"

"Why not?"

Garibaldi inclined his head. "That would mean a long trip into the city. How would they move fifteen tons of rock that far?"

Borel smiled. "See those trees?" He pointed at a line of scraggly willows standing out of the arid landscape. "They mark an underground aquifer. Five hundred years ago today's miserable trickle was a river. Natural at first, then made into a canal leading right into lake Texcoco. The Mexica would have floated the statue to Tenochtitlan on a raft."

Borel studied his questioners, noted the doubtful frowns, the narrow eyes. "Catalina — Dr. Delgado — she sent you here, right? Told you about me, about my dig?"

"Yes, she did."

"She thinks I'm crazy."

Traeger made a face. "She thinks you're . . . romantic."

Borel shook his head. "That woman . . . here, let me show you something."

He made a come-along gesture and led the trio under his site's canvas canopy and down a perilous stairway cut into the hard soil. There he pointed out the remains of a stone door frame decorated with pre-Columbian symbols.

"This look romantic?" he asked rhetorically, "or like the real deal?"

No door was in place within the frame. Perhaps there never was one. Instead, the American searchers were staring at a hollowed-out tunnel.

Borel pulled a cord on a small gasoline-powered generator to fire it up, threw a switch, and a line of lights dangling from the tunnel's low ceiling showed that the dig extended ten meters beyond the door frame. After that, darkness.

Garibaldi retreated from the doorway.

Sarzeau was quick to notice his edgy mood. "You feel it too, huh, Roman?"

"Oh yeah . . ."

Borel scratched his head. "Feel what? What are you talking about?"

Traeger pointed a finger at Sarzeau. "It's only fair to warn you, doc — Marianne's a witch."

Borel adopted an expression of profound disbelief. "She feels things?"

Sarzeau grinned. "Sometimes. Like now."

"Incredible."

"Roman here, he's not a full adept, but he gets nervous around stuff."

"What stuff? Come on, folks, so the Aztecs were bloodthirsty monsters — they're all dead now, *no problemo.*"

Garibaldi waved his hands around. "This isn't about the Aztecs, it's who might have influenced their art."

"Oh? Who are you people, anyway? Catalina was kind of vague."

Sarzeau didn't answer. She had thoughts of her own.

"Doctor Borel — you started a dig here when your colleagues and associates thought your judgment was, well, *clouded* at best. What made you do it? Why are you still at it? Can't be the stone chips and beads."

Borel folded his arms and toed a lump of dirt. "Hard to say, really." He paused, then mumbled, "Intuition?"

"Exactly!" Sarzeau punched him on the shoulder. "You're like my friend Roman here, sensitive to emanations."

The idea jolted Borel. "Ghosts? No thanks!"

"You heard about the starbots?"

Borel nodded slowly. "You're intelligence agents. CIA, right?"

"Close enough," said Sarzeau. "The starbots think their ancestors — the ones who were tinkering with our DNA — left something behind. We think so too, and we're here to find it."

▼

Sarzeau led the group into the tunnel, moving slowly to the far end.

"What do you feel?" she asked.

"It was stronger a few feet back," muttered Garibaldi.

"Hey, I noticed the same thing," added Borel. He was surprised by a nagging sense of discomfort, now that he was consciously aware of it.

They backtracked a couple of meters. Sarzeau put her hand against the packed dirt wall.

"How about now?"

Garibaldi and Borel both nodded.

"Yeah, me too," said Sarzeau.

"Next season," vowed Borel, "I'll recruit a bunch of under-grads, and we'll punch a hole here, see what we can see."

Sarzeau started clawing at the dirt wall. "Let's make it this sea-son. If I'm right, there's a door here, and a room beyond."

Soon dirt began falling away, revealing hints of a barrier.

"I'm surprised you didn't spot this already," said Garibaldi. "Where's your seismic gear?"

Borel was embarrassed. "Ask the Spofford Center for New World Underfunding."

He exited the tunnel, sorted through a pile of rusty tools in the anteroom, and returned with a long-handled rake.

"Here, let me . . ."

He gently raked the spot until an obvious portal was revealed.

"What is this stuff? Not rock, not brick . . ."

Sarzeau placed her hands on the slab and pushed with all her might. The portal cracked open, but refused to budge any further. A jet of air escaped from within, blowing out a cloud of dust carrying the dry odor of abandonment.

Borel felt his legs wobble, as if he had downed one too many tequila shots. "Looks like we've got a room here, ha-ha! Major discovery! Who's romantic now? Huh? Who?"

Back on the surface, Garibaldi opened up his satellite phone and made a call to NITCOM. The conversation went on for five minutes. When it was over he collapsed the phone's antenna and folded it up.

"I alerted HQ. General Congreve is talking with American TV & Appliance. They're going to send a service team."

Borel leaned against his rake to steady himself. "Service team? What is that?"

Garibaldi smiled. "Speed up your dig, doc."

45

GARIBALDI checked his watch: 8:30 pm, Central Standard Time in Mexico. The Sun was down, and the sky was black. He strolled a couple of hundred yards from Borel's dig site, out of the trees, over a crumbling stone wall, and onto the edge of Teotihuacan's main thoroughfare, the Avenue of the Dead. There he stopped to listen to the nighttime sounds: owls, crickets, cicadas, the yips of a coyote.

Gradually another sound separated itself from the noises of nocturnal wildlife; the monotonous hum of powerful airplane engines.

Garibaldi was equipped with a flashlight commandeered from Borel's dig. He aimed it into the sky and flicked it on and off in a rhythmic pattern.

The invisible airplane roared overhead. Thirty seconds later small red LEDs dotted the sky, fireflies competing with the stars. They belonged to U.S. Army Rangers descending from the airplane under parachutes that resembled soft-winged paragliders.

Garibaldi ran to the first man on the ground and helped him strip off his harness. The Ranger lit a flare and threw it into the avenue. Twenty-five of his squad mates homed in on the flare and touched down in carefully timed ten-second intervals. A few seconds after that, unmanned chutes deposited heavy pallets of gear that shook the Earth on landing.

The last man down removed his harness, gathered in his chute, and marched across the dry grass to Garibaldi.

"Hello, Mo," said the scientist. "Still the astronaut, I see. I thought you might join the party."

"Did you now?" replied General Upshaw with a broad grin. He shook Garibaldi's hand and smacked him on the back. "Help me get our operation organized and under cover."

▼

"What have we got here?" queried Upshaw, standing in Ari Borel's underground tunnel.

Sarzeau shrugged. "We think there's a good-sized room on the other side of this door. Don't laugh — Doctor Borel, Roman, and I all feel a presence."

"I'm not laughing," allowed Upshaw with a little bow, his way of signaling respect for Sarzeau's uncanny abilities.

"The door — or panel — we were able to move it about an inch, so maybe not, maybe there's no room, just . . . dirt."

Upshaw beckoned to one of his Rangers.

"Let's take a good look. Hugh? C-4?"

Captain Donaldson worked his way through the assembly carrying a stick of plastic explosive, which he molded against the putative door.

Borel's eyebrows shot up. "Good God! You're not going to use that in here, in my dig!"

Upshaw made a face. "Sorry, doc, but our military needs override your science tonight."

"The fuck not! This is Mexican property, we're here with the indulgence of the Mexican government. They've got rules!"

Donaldson hooked up the wires.

"Out of the tunnel, everyone. This is going to throw gravel everywhere and blow out your eardrums. Back, back!"

Borel made an attempt to yank the wires out of the putty-like explosive charge. Garibaldi grabbed his arm. A pair of Rangers sprang into action and hustled the archeologist out of the tunnel.

"Keep a close eye on our digger, men," ordered Upshaw.

When everyone was clear of the tunnel and back on the surface, Captain Donaldson connected up his pistol-grip detonator and pressed the trigger.

BOOM

The explosion punched the resisting door into the middle of a darkened room. Rock fragments ricocheted off the dig site walls and clattered against the canvas canopy above. A cloud of choking dust billowed out of the tunnel.

They waited for five minutes to let the place settle down. Then Garibaldi led the group back down to where the previously jammed door had given way to a yawning portal. He handed his borrowed flashlight back to Borel.

"Here you go, doc. Your dig, check it out. You don't need any undergrads."

Borel gave the group a bitter nod, turned on the flashlight, and ducked through the opening.

"You're welcome," said Garibaldi.

Rangers followed with powerful LED lights on tall tripods. Captain Donaldson turned on a small video camera and began recording their discovery.

"This looks just like Zimbabwe, like the inner rooms there," said Sarzeau, speaking in hushed awestruck tones.

The group was standing in another room fashioned by the starbots' alien ancestors. Flat walls covered in a plaster-like material. A table on which lay oddly formed metallic instruments. Shelves holding jars containing the dried-out residue of colorful liquids. A mural on the wall filled with symbols and diagrams. On another wall a stylized illustration of the alien inhabitants. And, in the middle of the room, a stone sarcophagus.

"Oh my God!" cried Borel. His resentment of the military was momentarily swept away by their stunning find. "Howard Carter had nothing on this!"

46

AFTER TWO HOURS of fruitless searching, nothing further was found. No more doors to open, no obvious reason to believe the area contained anything of value to the starbots.

Sarzeau examined the mural. "I still feel something. We've seen this sort of puzzle before. Nikki Traeger nodded agreement. She tried pressing various symbols in different orders and combinations without any result.

"Shit."

General Upshaw sat himself down on the sarcophagus.

"Here's a little story, people. Remember Rudy-Red-Nose, your talker bot? After we refused the starbot demand to hand him over, they sent out one of their spider bots. A big one, size of a golf cart, middle of the night. It attacked the trailer where we were trying to rev up your chatterbox. It managed to slice open the trailer door with its claws and cut up the guard pretty good before we were able to knock it out."

Garibaldi was shocked by the news. "Knock it out? How?"

Captain Donaldson grinned. "We don't want to use our wavers any more than necessary, in case the bots figure out our codes again. So we shot it."

"Shot it . . ."

"Yup, five rounds from a Glock works wonders. It shattered. The pieces bounced around like coals from a campfire and then turned to sand. Rudy-Red is safe."

Sarzeau sighed. "Nice story, but we're stalled out here. I can tell you there's something behind that mural, but we can't solve the puzzle or find any evidence of an opening."

"Story's not over," said Upshaw. "We managed to revive the little fella."

"No way," said Garibaldi.

Upshaw signaled to one of the Rangers. "And — we brought him along."

▼

A few minutes later Ranger specialists entered the tunnel carrying an aluminum case, from which they removed a small robot. Headless, armless, equipped only with two spindly legs, a red laser, and a row of light sensors arranged around its boxy torso.

"Maybe he can help us," said Upshaw.

"It might take a few minutes. His battery isn't in great shape, and we need to top up his charge."

The specialists placed the robot on a plastic pad under one of the work lights. They ran wires from the pad back to a heavy truck battery, connected everything up and began the charging procedure.

"This works?"

"Just like your iPhone, doc."

The process took ten minutes. Then, suddenly, Rudy sat up.

"Dark. Dark in box," he said.

"Sounds like you, doc," noted Traeger, "English teacher to the stars." Indeed, Garibaldi's vocal characteristics had rubbed off on the little talker bot.

The Rangers turned Rudy loose in the newly opened room, and he tottered around, giving everything a cursory look.

"My Lords lived here." He stopped beside the sarcophagus. "One remains."

He spun around and approached the mural on the far wall.

"Instructions," he said, turning this way and that to scan the mural with his laser. Then he returned to the tomb.

Rudy tilted to one side, freeing a foot. Using the appendage as a hand, he pressed a spot on the side of the sarcophagus, unlocking the lid with an audible *klik*.

"You help now," he tootled.

Rangers gathered to shove the lid aside. Ari Borel couldn't resist and joined the effort. With much groaning and heaving the lid moved aside, then toppled to the floor revealing a shriveled and leathery apparition.

"So that was one of the ancestors . . ." mused Traeger, snapping photographs.

"Not much to look at," said Garibaldi with a shudder.

The wide head was reduced to desiccated parchment drawn tightly over wide-set and empty eye sockets. Crumbled shards were all that remained of a skull.

"Just as well, I'm spooked as it is," added Upshaw.

Borel was fascinated. "Look, curved teeth. Put it all together, imagine some flesh to fill out the form, and you have . . ."

". . . Coatlicue," finished Sarzeau. She was shivering.

Rudy-Red-Nose was hopping up and down, attempting to join the body in the sarcophagus.

"What?"

"You help now," repeated the talker bot.

Borel rolled his eyes and picked him up. "I can't believe I'm doing this."

He gently deposited the little guy inside the stone tub. There Rudy thrashed around, kicking at the alien body, loosening its joints and shredding its leathery skin. He tilted onto one leg again, reached out with his other one, and scraped away an accumulation of debris.

"Found it!" he exclaimed.

Then he toppled over. His battery charge had expired.

Borel pulled a face mask over his nose and leaned into the sarcophagus.

"Get a photo, please. There's a button or lever in here. Looks like I can move it."

Traeger and Captain Donaldson snapped pictures.

"Okay, here goes."

Borel stuck a thumb down and pressed it against a small knob.

Garibaldi chuckled. "This is great. Only in the movies do prehistoric buttons operate prehistoric machinery."

"Better tell Rudy, he's the star of this show," said Sarzeau, pushing the immobilized talker bot into his arms.

The group steadied itself as a low grinding noise resonated through the room. An exhalation of dust puffed out of the mural, outlining a portal.

Borel, awestruck by the rapid progress his dig was making, progress that ordinarily took years to accomplish, shuffled dreamily across the room to the far wall.

"More photos, please."

He rubbed his hands together for luck and gingerly placed them on the mural.

"Going to give this section a shove now . . ."

He pushed. The area within the portal outline swung aside with a tooth-rattling squeal. Beyond it another room was revealed, this one small and dark.

▼

Lights were positioned. Documentary photos were taken. Borel peered inside. The walls were bare and the ceiling was low. The archeologist was forced to crawl on hands and knees to get inside.

"What's this?"

He was looking at an artifact fashioned from smooth grey metal. It was cubical, roughly a meter wide, tall, and deep. Strange symbols, like those on the mural, were engraved on the near side. Borel ran his hands over the surfaces. He could not detect apertures of any kind, but several small circles of darker material with a slippery texture were set into each side.

Garibaldi was holding off a case of the willies. "What about it? Feel anything in there?"

"Excitement!" came Borel's reply. "Too bad there's no Nobel Prize for archaeology! What we've got here — it's unique. Some kind of machinery, evidently."

Sarzeau peeked at the object Borel was describing. "I feel power. That thing, that cube — it's pumping out energy."

"Radioactivity? Is it hot?" worried Upshaw.

Captain Donaldson activated a compact Geiger counter. He held it in the air briefly, then reached into the tiny room and pressed it against the cube itself. "Not a trace, sir. Cold as ice."

"Anything but ghosts," mused Garibaldi. He dropped to his knees and crawled into the room, not much more than a closet really, for a good look at the prize.

"It's a machine, all right," he confirmed. "Notice the heavy knobs here along the base?"

He examined the cube's bottom edges. Each knob contained a hole. He stuck his fingers into one of them. "These are bolt holes. Big ones."

General Upshaw motioned to his Rangers. "Let's get that thing out of there."

The Ranger specialists buckled tiedown straps around the cube and hauled away. It emerged grudgingly into the outer room, where the entire expedition could get a view.

"Titanium," appraised Upshaw.

Borel scratched his head. "Any idea what it is?"

"Nope. But unless I miss my guess, this is what the starbots are looking for."

"I don't see any screws, no faceplates, no obvious way to check inside."

Captain Donaldson opened a pack and brought forth a laptop computer, packaged for industrial use, and an egg-shaped sensor on a USB cable.

"Ultrasound."

Garibaldi turned it on and stuck the sensor against one side of the cube. The group gathered around the laptop. What they saw were unidentifiable machine parts arrayed around a donut-shaped torus. The functionality was obscure.

Rangers hoisted the cube onto a fiberglass pallet, accidentally passing near the inert Rudy-Red-Nose. Suddenly the little talker bot woke up. Apparently drawn by magnetic attraction, he skidded across the floor to the cube. One of his legs fastened onto one of the artifact's dark circular spots. His red laser blazed and went out, extinguished by a power overload. He twisted himself around to address the group.

"A gift from my Lords to those who can find it," he warbled. *Annnxxxx . . .*

Then he blew up. Parts flew in all directions. Everyone ducked. A leg grazed Sarzeau's upraised hand as it flew by her face.

47

RESPONDING TO ORDERS from General Upshaw, the Army Ranger company inflated a large balloon shaped like a blimp, set a light flashing inside, and floated the thing high into the air on a stout woven tape. Soon it was a flashing beacon in the predawn sky.

At the dig site, other Rangers hauled the alien cube outside. There they tied it securely onto its pallet and wrapped it in sheets of foam, heavy black plastic, and canvas webbing.

Ari Borel watched the balloon go up with growing alarm. He turned to Upshaw.

"What are you doing?"

"Can't land a plane on the Avenue of the Dead, so we need to make a flying pickup. A tricked-out C-130 is going to grab that tether and yank our prize right off the ground."

Don't tell me you're thinking of stealing this thing."

"We're not stealing. This artifact wasn't made by native people or anyone else here on Earth. It isn't pre-Columbian, it's pre-human!"

"We're on Mexican soil. You understand? We have to notify the *Instituto Nacional.* Talk to Delgado, or her friend Garcia. They'll want to send people to take possession."

"No thank you, Doctor."

Nikki Traeger was equally disturbed. "Americans! Always the bastards!"

Garibaldi overheard her remark. "Hey, Borel is American. This is an American dig, right? Financed by Americans — the Spofford Center, ring a bell?"

Traeger wasn't buying. "But . . ."

"No buts. It's ours!"

Sarzeau heard the heat and took up a stance near her colleague.

Garibaldi didn't notice.

"We can't leave the secrets of the universe to a bunch of ridiculous Mexicans," he insisted.

"Roman!" yelped Sarzeau. Her face was red. "What a thing to say!"

Garibaldi gave her a guilty look. He shrugged. "Treasures are treacherous. Welcome to reality, Sarzeau."

Upshaw watched his men harness the cube and its pallet to the tape dangling from the balloon. He nodded satisfaction and thumbed a switch on his satellite phone.

"Hello, NITCOM — the basketball has bounced. Looking for a three-point shooter. Send soonest. Out."

At NITCOM HQ, General Congreve gave the order to dispatch an MC-130 equipped with a surface-to-air pickup device to central Mexico.

At almost the same moment, a surveillance team staffer called to report the possibility of aerial activity coming from the Quonset hut. Once again the roof was opening up.

Congreve observed the giant hatchway through binoculars. After a few heartbeats, a large wingless starbot ship leaped into the sky. It was gone from sight in no time.

NORAD failed to track the bogey, and its radar operators could provide no information on its trajectory or destination.

"God *damn* it!" bellowed Congreve.

▼

On Teotihuacan's Avenue of the Dead, Rangers readying the packed-up cube for aerial pickup were distracted by a small crab-like robot angling around their work area. A tiny green headlight on the bot's nose gave it away in the dull predawn shadows.

"What the fuck!" squawked one of the Rangers, pointing at the thing.

"Holy shit!" cried his partner. "What is it?"

Upshaw and Garibaldi raced to have a look.

"Oh my God — a bot! How did it get here?"

The answer to Upshaw's question was: espionage. Once the starbots lost their small satellite, they became aware that humans might know more than they did. They soon learned that NIT-COM airplanes started their missions out of Luke Air Force base near Phoenix and took steps to figure out their destinations.

The C-130J that deposited Upshaw and his detachment of Army Rangers on the ground in Mexico had a stowaway that spent a long flight attached to one of the cargo pallets. When the Rangers hit their chutes, so did the stowaway.

By the time humans discovered the thing, it had already radioed its position back to the starbot base and was performing a reconnaissance mission for its masters.

Upshaw marched across the avenue with an M-16 in hand. He let the little robot scuttle close, then brought the butt of the rifle down on its back with a crushing *thud.*

"How long until our truck arrives overhead?"

Garibaldi checked his watch. "Another hour, Mo."

"Captain Donaldson!"

"Here, sir."

"Get your men ready for combat. Who knows who gets here first."

As it happened, the starbot ship arrived within minutes, settling slowly onto the wide expanse of Teotihuacan's main thoroughfare, a couple of hundred yards north of the human position.

A long arm formed at the near end of the vehicle. A toothy digger emerged from the arm and began to tear up the ground, feeding dirt and debris into an aperture that cracked open on the vehicle's flank. As the humans watched, it rumbled and shook. Waves rippled along the shiny surface, which now appeared to be flexible, and the ship stunned its observers by doubling in size.

"Okay, that gets a wow!" gulped Traeger. She leveled her camera and cranked off a dozen photos.

Captain Donaldson formed up the Rangers. They separated themselves into a wide phalanx and advanced upon the starbot ship, assault rifles, grenades, and bazookas at the ready.

The ship paid no heed until the troops were drawing near. Then a second arm jutted out from the shiny body. It projected a bright blue laser beam over the Rangers and over Nikki Traeger, who was boldly marching alongside, alternately documenting the soldiers and the ship's behavior with her Nikon.

The laser-wielding arm retracted into the ship's hull, and a different arm appeared, smaller, with a tiny nozzle on the end.

Bap

A tiny pellet flew out of the nozzle. It drilled through Captain Donaldson's flak jacket and exploded in his chest. He coughed, stumbled, and pitched over, dead before he hit the ground.

Upshaw ran forward, grabbed the captain's bazooka, and let fly. The rocket tore into the starbot ship and blew a hole in its shiny surface. A hole that quickly sealed itself.

Bap Bap Bap Bap Bap Bap Bap Bap Bap

Now the alien cannon whipped back and forth firing its tiny explosive pellets at the Rangers, nailing each in turn.

Upshaw dove to the ground and crawled away to the edge of the avenue, holding one leg, where a pellet had shattered the tibia.

Traeger was not so lucky. Without a flak jacket to stop it, the pellet aimed in her direction went right through her chest and failed to explode. But it nicked her heart on the way, and she fell, as dead as the rest.

Garibaldi grabbed Sarzeau by her golden ponytail and yanked her down behind the cube.

"Oh no, no, no, no . . ." he groaned.

The remaining Rangers fanned out among the low trees on each side of the avenue. While waiting for the right moment to renew their attack they churned out a fusillade of defensive fire. Assault weapons rattled, and sparks danced harmlessly across the enemy ship's hull. Grenades flew and exploded without effect. Bazooka rockets streamed out of the foliage, each one punching a hole in the ship's flanks, and each hole promptly sealed itself.

"Don't we have any of Holly's wave guns?" wailed Sarzeau.

"In one of the packs, probably . . . somewhere."

They crouched in place. After a couple of minutes the unmistakable whine of turboprop engines reached their ears.

"Shit, that plane? It's going to snag this pallet, haul it away, and we'll be sitting ducks."

But no — as the plane approached the flashing balloon, silhouetted against the pale sky, it's fuselage erupted with fiery explosions. It banked left, missed the balloon, and lumbered away to the south.

Now a section of the starbot ship opened into a portal, and out slid replicas of the dead Rangers who were previously scanned by the blue laser.

Garibaldi watched with a sinking heart. "Oh my God — *sandos!* So that's how they do it!"

Sarzeau peeked around the edge of the bundled-up cube.

"Not like our old pal Jim Lockwood. And there's Nikki. She's one of them!"

Garibaldi smacked Sarzeau's butt. "Gotta jet, Sarzeau."

He sprang to his feet and made a dash toward Borel's dig site. Sarzeau counted to three, jumped up, and followed him.

They dove under the trees just as a dozen pellets whizzed by their ears, snapping leaves off the branches.

"What now?"

"Let's get underground. The bots want that cube, not us."

They steeled themselves for their next move, then stopped to listen. The sound of the cargo plane faded away, and a faraway rumble echoed through the ancient city.

"That was our plane," said Garibaldi.

He wasn't wrong. The pilots of the crippled MC-130 fought to keep it airborne, but it ran into the lower slopes of Mount Popocatépetl, a huge stratovolcano south of the city, and exploded.

The sando army roamed along the avenue, firing their pellet guns into the trees, killing half a dozen Rangers as they advanced toward the cube.

One of the surviving soldiers managed to hit the sando version of Traeger with a rocket, blowing her to smithereens, but she soon reappeared, sliding out of the starbot ship's portal, fully restored and fully armed.

Garibaldi was appalled. He stood, grabbed Sarzeau's hand, and dragged her to her feet. "Gotta go, gotta go now. No way to win this skirmish."

Traeger was first to reach the cube. She raised a hand in triumph, summoning the ship, which grew a set of wheels and lumbered forward to capture the prize.

Down in the dig site anteroom, Garibaldi rummaged through the packs stashed there. He emptied several and threw them aside before he finally got his hands on a prototype waver.

"Hey!" he exclaimed. He dug around, found a second one and tossed it to Sarzeau.

"Let's go — into the tunnel."

"I don't know — dark in there."

"Dark is good."

They crept into the narrow passage, where they met Ari Borel, who was quivering with fear — or possibly rage.

"How is it up there? Are the bots gone yet?"

"Not yet."

"They just want my artifact, right? I mean, why else would they attack?"

"Take it easy, doc. We've got these microwave guns. They dissolve the bad guys." Sarzeau hefted her weapon. "We'll be safe in here," she promised.

Borel stared at the shadowy waver. "Give me that!" He ripped it out of Sarzeau's hands. His eyes were bulging. "They cannot be allowed to steal my cube!"

Borel marched out of the tunnel and up the dirt stairs, pointing the waver ahead of himself. Just outside the tent he encountered the duplicated Nikki Traeger.

"Hey there, Lady. Look what I've got."

He attempted to activate the weapon, but unfamiliarity with its operation made him fumble with the trigger.

"Who is down there?" demanded Traeger.

"Um, science guy and that witch."

"Thank you."

Traeger lifted her pellet gun and punched two holes in Borel. Little explosions rearranged his internal organs, and he fell backwards into the dig.

Traeger boldly descended the dirt stairs and turned toward the darkened tunnel. "Marianne? Garibaldi? You in there? It's me, Nikki."

She was about to send a cautionary stream of pellets into the passageway when Garibaldi stood up with his waver running.

Traeger dropped her gun. She brought her hands to her face. She started shaking all over.

"Ah-ah-ah-ah-ah-ah . . ." she moaned.

Then she exploded in a blizzard of sparkling particles.

▼

Outside, the duplicated Rangers dragged the alien cube, already packed for transport, toward the waiting starbot ship. An opening on the ship's flank gaped wide as the precious cargo drew near.

Garibaldi and Sarzeau watched their progress from the conceal-ment of the trees, where they stumbled upon Upshaw in a hollow under one of them. His dark face was grey. His teeth were chat-tering. They noticed blood staining the grass under his leg.

Sarzeau whipped off her belt. Garibaldi laced it around Upshaw's thigh as a makeshift tourniquet and tightened it down.

"Thanks," grunted the wounded soldier.

"Shh, Mo, not over yet," said Sarzeau.

She pointed at the sandos who were busy loading the ancient cube into the starbot ship. Once it was safely onboard, the former humans backed away. They watched the ship rise silently into the air without any need of wings, tilt skyward, and zoom away to the north.

Upshaw tried to sit up and catch a glimpse. A stabbing pain ran up his shattered leg, causing him to groan.

The sandos turned toward the sound.

"There they are! Get them!"

They shambled toward the humans, who shrank down on the ground.

"They look wobbly," hissed Upshaw.

"Not that wobbly!" countered Garibaldi.

Weapons were raised on both sides. Sarzeau readied her waver. The sandos aimed their pellet guns.

By now the starbot ship was streaking through the upper atmos-phere, and its power to sustain a combat squad was fading with every mile traveled. Long before the ship reached the American border, and just before the starbot slaves reached the last remain-ing members of the NITCOM team, they all dissolved into little piles of shimmering sand.

48

WHAT'S the count? How many did we lose, Mo?" queried General Congreve.

"Nineteen rangers, including Captain Donaldson," replied Upshaw, who was snugged up in a wheelchair with his leg elevated in a cast. He grimaced. "Plus the archeologist Borel, and our journalist friend, Nikki Traeger."

Congreve acknowledged the losses with a grim nod.

"Terrorist raid, that's what we're calling it."

Mexican police had arrived at the dig site in Teotihuacan soon after the action concluded, dispatched by numerous hair-raising tales and complaints. They counted the bodies, assessed the damage, and threatened to hold the American survivors on charges. Walter Melrose, in his first real test as the new Secretary of State, managed to negotiate their release without mentioning the starbots, their ancestors, or the mysterious cube.

Now Upshaw, Garibaldi, and Sarzeau were back in the NIT-COM command post being debriefed on their mission.

Tom Wagstaff was standing by with a protective arm wound tight around Sarzeau's waist. He had a question:

"Did the cube show any details? Like power sockets?"

Garibaldi scowled. "No sockets, no lids, no faceplates or screws or openings of any kind. He snapped his fingers. "But there were knobs all around the base. Big ones, with big bolt holes."

Wagstaff picked up a pile of photo prints from the map table and leafed through them. "Take a look at this," he said.

The photograph he referenced was taken by Sarzeau on her foray to rescue him and their son. It showed the underground starbot factory and what appeared to be a spaceship's hull section under construction. Wagstaff tapped the print.

"The Lockwood sando claimed his bot buddies were building

an interstellar ship. See the wires dangling there? And those big bolts protruding from the platform underneath?"

"Okay . . ."

"Well, that's got to be the engine room — those bolts are engine mounts — and now they have the engine," said Wagstaff.

"At no small cost to us," added Sarzeau.

"If we don't act," continued Wagstaff, "pretty soon they'll be using it to jet out of Dodge."

Garibaldi tightened his hands into fists. "I want that engine."

Congreve waved his arms to call a timeout. "Slow down, everyone. I can't act without orders from the Commander-in-Chief, you know that."

Barney Wyatt was only half listening, because he was on a call from the White House. He handed his phone to Congreve.

"President Fairbanks on the line for you, General."

"Mr. President, good to hear your voice."

Or maybe not so good. Fairbanks was in an angry mood.

"Barney tells me you lost all our troops down there in Mexico."

"Not quite all, sir."

"Don't quibble! It's a disaster. I've been sitting with the Cabinet, the National Security Council, members of Congress, and the Joint Chiefs, all the ding-dong day. Everyone's on board. Those damn starbots have to be stopped."

"Yes, sir, I understand, sir. There are some, however, who will be very upset if we take them out."

Fairbanks snorted. "You mean Secretary Rutledge. *Former* secretary!"

"And the Australian prime minister. They have developed quite a following."

"I don't give a good goddamn." The President paused. Congreve could hear him talking to some assistant in the Oval Office.

"Sir — ?"

"Tell you what, General — we have our *casus belli,* and I hereby authorize you to remove the existential starbot threat by whatever means you deem necessary. How's that?"

"Very good, sir."

"I'll wire the order. Barney will have it, and I will take full responsibility. If whatever you've got in mind goes south, you can hand my ticket to that nosy woman — what's her name? Broke all the news? — let her tar and feather me in public."

"Nikki Traeger. She's dead, Mr. President."

"Oh? Hand it to *The New York Times* then, I don't care."

"Yes, sir. Concrete proposal coming your way ASAP."

He put down the phone, moved to the window, stared thoughtfully at the wrecking yard.

"You said that the sandos all decomposed when the ship departed. What about it, Mo?"

"That's right. They don't handle power the way we do."

Congreve nodded. "And we know — assume, anyway, without contradiction — that whatever they're up to underneath that Quonset hut gets its juice from the Palo Verde Nuclear Generating Station. That right?"

"Very probable. The brownouts and all."

Congreve rubbed his hands together.

"Get me the mayor of Phoenix on the line. Better plug in the governor too."

▼

"Shutter Palo Verde? You must be out of your mind, General." The mayor of Phoenix was outraged by the idea. "We've got hospitals running, airports, traffic signals, supermarket freezers, to say nothing of private homes. Imagine Phoenix without air conditioning, for the love of God. You can't do it."

"Governor? What's your view?" asked Congreve.

"Well, sir, I was kind of hoping we'd get to be friends with our heavenly visitors. Kind of hoping they'd turn out to be angels, if you know what I mean."

"I do. But be aware, if we add up the totals, that little band of bots has already murdered fifty of your fellow Americans. They're cold-blooded killers."

"If you say so, and it's a tragedy. Of course, we had more than three hundred murders among regular human beings in Arizona last year, don't forget."

"Duly noted. I'm asking, will you authorize a nuclear shut-down, Governor? It's key to our strategy."

"I can't really do that. Atomic plants aren't like your TV set, you can't just turn 'em off. I would need a higher authority to take any action on that score."

"I understand. Thank you for speaking with me."

Congreve slammed his phone down on the map table.

"Barney!"

"General?"

"Get me the White House."

▼

Congreve apprised President Fairbanks of his plans and his problems implementing them. The President promised a word with the Secretary of Energy, the Arizona governor, and the mayor of Phoenix.

The outcome of the spirited discussion that ensued yielded a compromise. For exactly one-half hour, starting after sunset, the Palo Verde nuclear plant would reduce its electrical output and re-route all of its juice eastward to El Paso and San Antonio. Ten minutes before H-hour, critical systems managers in Arizona would be notified to take precautionary measures.

"Precautionary measures? Tip the enemy?"

"Best I can do, General," advised a weary President. "Be happy. Do your job. Rid us of those turbulent robots."

▼

General Congreve considered his limited assets — twenty microwave guns, three M1A1 tanks, two M114 howitzers on wheels, but only a dozen special forces personnel, whose numbers were severely depleted in the disastrous expedition to Mexico. Like any officer leading men into battle, he wished he had more weaponry, and a lot more troops. But he privately concluded that he had enough of each to inflict some serious shock and awe on the robotic rascals inside Stone Valley Scrap & Salvage. Inside the *wrecking yard* — he savored the term.

"We're really going to wreck that yard," he vowed and called for volunteers to fill the ranks. Holzgraf, Garibaldi, Wyatt, two cooks, and a state policeman opted in and dressed for combat.

Tom Wagstaff was restrained from joining up by his wife, who threatened to kill him herself if he so dared.

"You've done enough, babe," declared Sarzeau. "Gabe loves having a father, so we're going to watch from the sidelines."

To ease his conscience, Wagstaff drew a detailed map of the Quonset hut layout for the attackers to study.

The question of civilian casualties was raised. A small town had mushroomed into existence near the wrecking yard after the starbot presence was detected. What if the attack failed? What if the bots countered by laying waste to everything?

"If we shoo everyone out, the bad guys may take warning," advised Upshaw.

A decision was made: all curious alien-watchers had to go, but not until H-hour minus ten, when the Arizona power warning would be issued.

Congreve spent some time finalizing his order of battle. None of his ordnance would move into position until the attack was underway. First, Rangers with wavers would cut through the perimeter fence and stealthily dissolve as many bots and sandos as possible before heavy artillery bombarded the starbot base, which was sure to stir up a hornet's nest.

Elite soldiers would then move into the hut, locate the factory, dissolve its workers, demolish the spaceship under construction, and recover the precious cube.

"Precious *engine,*" emphasized Garibaldi.

Congreve consulted the NITCOM brain trust, and they all signed off.

"Just remember, flak jackets won't stop those explosive little pellets," cautioned Upshaw. "So use those wrecks for cover."

▼

H-hour minus ten:

All over Arizona, state and local officials were being warned of an imminent power outage. State police officers started moving spectators out of the wrecking yard viewing area, ignoring the strident complaints. Eighteen men wearing full combat gear and camouflaged face paint spread out along the perimeter fence facing the Quonset hut doorway. They carried the latest wave guns in addition to conventional M-16 assault rifles strapped across their backs. Crews took up positions in the tanks and around the howitzers.

H-hour:

All the floodlights along the perimeter fence went dark. So did all lights in the Quonset hut. Likewise the lights and gadgetry of the NITCOM operation.

The Rangers started cutting holes in the perimeter fence, then stopped. Brom-Kat-Su came flying out of the hut, roaring loudly through his built-in loudspeaker.

"General Congreve! Talk to me! We must talk!"

Congreve stepped out of the command post and strode boldly up to the wrecking yard perimeter. He was working hard to appear calm and relaxed.

"Yes, Director. Um, Glorious Brom. How can I help you?"

"Restore power. Immediately. Restore immediately or there will be consequences."

"What sort of consequences . . . exactly?"

"You're a military man. Details? You don't need them. Your operation will suffer terrible losses."

"I suppose you mean that as a threat. Is that how I should understand you?"

The latest edition of the Lockwood sando strode up beside his leader to soften the ultimatum. "Please understand this, General," he pleaded. "Restore power or many will die. Many, on both sides. A terrible tragedy. Do you want that?"

"They will not be resurrected," vowed his starbot overlord.

"I like the concept," replied Congreve. "Death without resurrection."

He made a casual salute, the signal for three Rangers to stand up with their wavers firing.

"Nooo . . !"

Brom spun his hoverboard around and dodged back to the shelter of his Earthly headquarters before the beams could take effect. Lockwood was not so quick. He staggered. He shed particles in a frenzied dance. He dissolved.

"So long, Captain."

The improvised combat team poured through the gap in the fence, advancing rapidly toward the Quonset hut, weaving between the car wrecks.

Half a dozen sandos, the confused replicas of wrecking yard workmen, slowly fanned out of the hut's doorway, brandishing pellet guns uncertainly.

Rangers popped up from several different positions and bathed them in microwaves. All were reduced to sandy granules before they could take action.

Now the soldiers moved cautiously to the hut's main doorway. Garibaldi peeled a satchel charge off his back, Holzgraf pulled a lanyard to light a fuse, and threw it into the hut itself. A moment later a tremendous explosion crumpled the hut's walls. The roof sagged downward.

Inside, at the far end of the hut, another group of sandos had a pellet cannon set up. Three Rangers went down before tanks and howitzers let loose, blowing the pellet cannon and its operators away.

Wyatt shouldered a bazooka and fired it down the stairs. The explosion knocked him flat and singed his eyebrows.

The team crouched down while heavy artillery sent another volley into the hut. Then they scampered down the stairs, looking for the starbots' underground factory. A raging firestorm halted them. Wyatt's bazooka blast had ignited the used motor oil reservoir, and it was burning hot.

It took several minutes — minutes that seemed like hours — to get a squad of firefighters to join them and put their foaming extinguishers to work. After the choking oil smoke dissipated they lowered their night vision goggles over their eyes and pressed on, following the route laid out by Tom Wagstaff.

The factory was not an easy target. The entrance was held by a number of working sandos, and the pellets from their guns flew every which way, exploding on the walls and ceiling, forcing the NITCOM team to retreat into the stairwell.

"What now? What do we do?" bleated Garibaldi.

The twenty-something Ranger in charge of the assault studied the obvious amateurs at his elbow. "Hey, Pop, who are you guys, anyway?"

Garibaldi was forty-five. He acknowledged the generation gap with a shrug. "Cube recovery, Son. The reason you're here."

Wyatt hooked his helmet over the muzzle of his M-16 and

extended it into the open . . .

Ping Ping Ping

. . . and drew it back, riddled with holes.

"Oh boy."

Garibaldi fetched a stainless steel mirror from his kit. He aimed it around the corner.

"Whoa!"

The sandos in the factory doorway were staggering around, and one by one they dissolved without human assistance.

"You poor guys — oh dear, power outage!" cackled Wyatt. He was preparing a satchel charge, but Garibaldi put a hand out to stop him.

"No, no, we can't blow the place."

"And why not?" hissed Wyatt.

"The cube. 'Nuff said?"

Wyatt nodded unhappily.

"All quiet on the Western Front, you think?" asked Holzgraf.

"It's dark in there, power's been off for ten minutes, maybe more. We see the effects. Let's go! Go! Go! Go!"

One by one they dodged through the doorway, relying on their night vision goggles to see the way.

But Brom-Kat-Su, starbot-in-chief, was not yet reduced to sand. A cable ran from his body to one of the circular pads on the cube, powering him and one of his flexible arms, which now ended in a lethal purple laser. He sprayed the beam back and forth at his attackers, who ducked and tumbled to safety behind sections of his unfinished spaceship.

"Stay down."

"Down! Check!"

"Should we take a chance? Hit him hard?"

"Don't be an idiot. The cube!"

"Oh right, the cube. I give it one minute. This thing I'm hiding behind is already dissolving. I'm going to blow that bot away."

"Absolutely not."

Sounds of the debate carried across the factory floor to big Brom, who was listening intently.

"My human cousins should stand up. Let them come to me in counsel. Let us forge a truce!"

"Hear that?" scoffed Holzgraf. "A truce! World peace is ours!"

"Last week I might have listened," snarled Wyatt. "Not tonight!"

A pair of orange membranes materialized over Brom's forward-facing eyes.

"I see you hiding. It is not what dignity requires. Come forth!"

The massive robot took a step toward the crouching humans. Then another. Garibaldi angled his mirror to watch the advance.

"He's found us, guys!"

Brom took another step. There were the humans, coming into sharp focus. He aimed his laser, activated the beam.

But nothing happened. Brom's final step yanked the cable connecting him to the alien cube free, cutting off his power supply.

The big bot tottered. A tinny gurgling noise issued from the speaker mounted in his torso.

Gah-gah-gah-gah-gah

Like the unfinished spaceship itself, and like his minions, the glorious Brom-Kat-Su dissolved into sandy debris.

"Dust to dust, eh, Mr. Starbot!"

The only thing left intact within the ruined factory was the mysterious cube.

▼

With the help of the special forces contingent, Garibaldi, Holzgraf, and Wyatt strapped the alien cube onto a wooden pallet. Like pallbearers with a coffin, they hoisted the thing onto their shoulders and staggered up the concrete stairway.

Partway up, lights flickered overhead. Wyatt checked his watch.

"Shit, our half-hour is up."

Indeed. Technicians at The Palo Verde Nuclear Generating Station were methodically re-routing their power onto the grid it normally served. The process of testing and validating hundreds of circuits was hit and miss.

"Eyes wide, guys," said Holzgraf. "Who knows what crazy bot stuff is still in working order."

As the group topped the stairs, the lights went out again. They deposited their alien burden on the ground. Soldiers hauled it away toward a waiting jeep.

The perimeter lights blinked on, off, on again.

"Hey!"

In a far corner of the ruined Quonset hut, one of the starbot fabricators was still operating. It regurgitated a new batch of sandos while the Rangers and ITF group watched with open mouths. In no time, pellets were flying from their handguns.

"Take cover!"

One of the Rangers bravely aimed his wave gun at the newly hatched combatants, but was slow on the trigger. Down he went as several pellets exploded in his chest.

Garibaldi peered out from behind a fallen section of Quonset hut roofing.

"Oh my God — these things look just like the men they killed in Mexico."

Holzgraf raised his wave gun over the crate he was hiding behind and pressed the trigger.

Garibaldi observed through a hole in the sheet metal protecting him. "One down! Two! Three! Way to go, Guy!"

Wyatt rolled out from behind the twisted remains of an industrial air compressor and let loose a burst of M-16 fire. Two of the remaining sandos cracked open like ceramic vases and collapsed.

The lights flickered and cycled off again as Palo Verde engineers sweated to restore electrical integrity.

Holzgraf yanked the fuse on the team's remaining satchel charge and tossed it into the darkness. The explosion blew debris up through the open roof and out the doorway, buzzing right past the heads of the human forces. In the fireball they could see sandos disintegrating.

All but one.

Holzgraf drilled it with a burst from his wave gun.

"No effect, Guy!" yelped Garibaldi. "What's wrong with your waver?"

"Maybe they changed the code again. I would have."

Finally the lights came on and stayed on, casting steady shadows into the Quonset hut wreckage.

The last remaining sando looked back at the starbot fabricator, which was dissolving even as power was restored. It looked at the pellet gun in its hand, watched it melt away.

"Damn."

It raised its arms, which remained intact, high overhead and took a step toward the humans huddling near the Quonset hut entrance.

"Don't shoot!"

Garibaldi jerked himself upright.

"Guns down, everyone!" he shouted.

He peered intently into the shadows at the figure swaying toward him.

"Christ almighty! Is that you, Traeger?"

"Once upon a time," replied the sando, "in another life."

49

THE NITCOM brain trust held a debriefing within hours of their big victory. President Fairbanks and his cabinet tuned in by video. The starbots were destroyed. The mysterious cube was recovered.

"Congratulations to the entire NITCOM team," enthused the President.

"What about our Mexican friends?" inquired Secretary Melrose. "They're going to want a piece of the action."

Congreve was about to make the case for possession, but he was overridden by the President himself.

"Christ, Wally, you sound like that wimp Rutledge," he said. "The alien object, engine, or whatever you call it, is not of human origin. And we did not transport it out of Mexican territory, that right, General?"

"Right you are, sir."

"The starbots did us that favor. And we lost good men — and women — in the process. We'll be keeping the cube. It's ours now."

"Gentlemen," continued Melrose, "let me just say, for the record, that this is the sort of diplomatic problem that spawns generations of distrust among allies. Sure this is our best course of action?"

The President wasn't deterred. "I hear you, Wally, got a big headache coming, I know. Throw 'em a bone — they can appoint one of their scientists to join us here, help us figure it all out."

"Without any authority, I hope," worried Garibaldi.

"Of course not!" said the President.

With that snippet of cynical *realpolitik* out of the way, the session turned to cleanup chores. All agreed that the cube was a state secret. All agreed that every last grain of sparkling sand should be found and incinerated. Efforts to discover any and all remaining extraterrestrial bushes should be redoubled. Satellite missions were proposed for the purpose. The Immigration Task Force was given a new charter.

▼

When the session ended, a contingent of NITCOM's brain trust gathered outside a trailer that served as Operation Welcome Wagon's stockade.

"When we go in there, remember — it's not really Traeger we'll be talking to," warned Upshaw.

"More like a damn starbot spy," nodded Wyatt.

"That's right," added Sarzeau. "We need to be cautious."

Inside, sitting in a hard-backed chair, manacled to stanchions welded into the wall behind her, was a near-perfect recreation of Nicolette Traeger, now the one remaining representative of starbot civilization.

"Should we still call you Nikki?" wondered Sarzeau. She was straining to get a feel for the entity in front of her, but the sando's emanations were vague and neutral.

"Call me anything you want. I still think of myself as Traeger."

Uncertain nods from the group. All were astonished by the sando's resemblance to the departed reporter, and all were creeped out by the subtle differences: skin texture just a little too smooth; fingers just a little too long; eyes just a little too bright; voice just a little too warm.

"Anything human in your noggin? Besides your name, I mean?" asked Garibaldi.

"I speak English. Give me a camera, I know how to take a newsworthy photograph."

Polite grunts among the visitors, pretending to grasp something that made all of their skins crawl.

"We were wondering," said Upshaw, "why you didn't dissolve

when the power failed."

"We have a better fabricator on the base than in the ship. Superior quality control. On top of that . . . a special effort was made. Special method. Like me or not, I'm permanent."

Sarzeau tapped a foot. "You're a sando now, Nikki. If you had one of those pellet guns, you'd kill us where we stand, is that right?"

Traeger smiled. She shook her head. "The fighting is over. You have our treasure, congratulations on that. And I still feel like a person" — she touched the close-cut halo of wavy threads atop her head — "as in, how's my hair look?"

"And you aren't affected by our wavers," noted Chow.

"Not the ones you were using."

"You changed the code again."

"It became necessary. Humans are quick, humans are clever."

"We could fool around, try new combos on you . . ." speculated Holzgraf.

"Please don't."

Upshaw raised a hand to stop that line of thought.

"Okay. Tell us why we shouldn't," he said.

"Well, as usual, I know something you don't. The starbots have another ship coming. Be here in umpty-umpteen years or so, with bots on board. My job? I'll be the designated go-between."

"You? A fucking go-between!" puffed Wyatt.

"Kat-Su ambassador. That sounds better," amended the sando.

"Even though," growled Sarzeau, "you killed Ari Borel."

"Yes I did. I did, and I can't deny it. I was killed first, remember. Casualties of war, they happen."

"We are inclined to be merciful," said Upshaw. "But for now you're a prisoner — P.O.W. — you understand that, right?"

"Where will you put me?" She produced a metallic grin. "Guantanamo?"

"Yet to be determined," said Wyatt.

"I can wait. Wait forever if need be. Give me a few hours with my fronds dangling in the Sun now and then, and I'm all yours."

Outside, Sarzeau detoured into one of the portable bathrooms and consulted a mirror.

"Whiskeyjack! Are we safe with this woman, Traeger? Can we trust her? I mean, the thing she turned into?"

The smoky demon's blue eyes flickered.

You don't need to trust her. Make use of her.

"Even though she's dangerous?"

I'm dangerous. You're dangerous. Thinking beings are all dangerous.

"What about the ship she talked about? Is it real . . ?"

But Whiskeyjack didn't know or didn't care to answer. He disappeared, and Sarzeau swore a string of oaths.

▼

Holzgraf and Chow approached General Upshaw, who looked to be their boss into the indefinite future.

"What about *The Tour?*" queried Chow.

"What about it?"

"What if Nikki isn't the only starbot survivor? Five other people spent hours in the starbot base at Lockwood's invitation, remember?"

"Your point?"

"Well, we zapped Sarzeau and Wagstaff and their kid. We know they're clean. But the rest . . ."

"You think . . ."

"Jim Lockwood actually *became* one of them," noted Holzgraf. "Slowly, a complete transformation . . . until we zapped him a few times, at least. We never guessed. The other sandos, here and everywhere, were replicas, manufactured like we make cars. And we found the real human corpses, so we know. But what if our tourists were infected somehow, like Lockwood?"

Upshaw was mildly disturbed by the possibility.

"What makes you think so?"

"How did the bots know our missions flew out of Luke Air Force Base? How did they get their tracker on that C-130?"

"You claiming they had a spy?"

"May have had."

"Those little bots were pretty smart. They could have attached themselves to a jeep right here at the wrecking yard, and jumped to the plane later," reasoned Upshaw.

Chow nodded. "Sure. But as a precaution, we want to test the tourists."

She produced a pistol-sized wave gun and handed it to Upshaw, who gave it a close examination.

"This is your tester?"

She and Holzgraf both nodded. "Our latest model."

"Pretty slick, I have to say."

He handed the gun back and studied the engineer and biologist with knitted brows.

"You don't look like spies, so watch your butts."

They found Barney Wyatt in the smoking ruins of the Stone Valley Scrap & Salvage yard, fending off the protests of the yard's angry owner, who wanted compensation. When Holzgraf leveled the new waver at the national security adviser, he grinned and raised his hands in surrender.

"Good idea, you guys. But, hey, I'm innocent."

Zannnggg

Sure enough, he was still an ordinary human being. The microwaves failed to muss his hair, let alone dissolve him.

"Nice to know you're you, Barney."

They bumped fists.

Garibaldi was hiking down the NITCOM operation's temporary main street towing a roll-around suitcase, grateful to be pulling up stakes like everyone else, when Chow and Holzgraf caught up with him.

Zaaappp

He too passed their test.

A flight on Southwest Airlines deposited Chow and Holzgraf in the California Bay Area. A call to the University of California in Berkeley told them that Professor Weatherall was not at her desk, and instead might be found on top of Mount Hamilton at the Lick Observatory, where she was on the hunt for planets outside our solar system.

They rented a car at the airport, crossed the bay, drove down to San Jose and then twenty miles up a winding road to the observatory on its suburban mountain peak, forty-two hundred feet above the sprawling cities of Northern California.

At three o'clock in the afternoon, with the Sun high overhead, they found their quarry standing outside the Automated Planet Finder telescope smoking a cigarette.

"Hey, Nancy, anything happening on our favorite exoplanet?"

"Well hello, you two." Weatherall stamped out her cigarette. "What brings you way up here?"

"We're on vacation. You know, until the next emergency."

"Still working for Mo Upshaw?"

"Yeah."

"Me too. But meanwhile, my department's got a bead on a planet a lot like ours only thirty-five light-years away" — she pointed into the sky — "right over there."

"Inhabited? Let's hope they call before they knock on our door."

"That would be the polite thing."

"So . . . we were wondering, would you be willing to take a

little test?"

Weatherall stepped back from the pair. "What kind of test?"

"We're hoping you're an ordinary human, and we want to prove it."

"Good God, you don't think . . ."

"Not really, but we want to check."

Weatherall did a little turn for them. "I didn't get a cost of living raise this year. Makes me feel pretty human."

Chow brought up her compact wave gun and pulled the trigger.

Zooowww

Nothing. Weatherall was still Weatherall, glowering at them. "Satisfied?"

Holzgraf nodded sheepishly. "You look good to us."

Chow came forward and embraced her. "Sorry for the doubts. Theoretical only, you understand."

"Mmm. Tell Mo I'll get him for this."

They nodded, anxious to get away from the awkward moment.

Weatherall stopped them with an afterthought. "I'm a saint, kids, but be sure to test that guy Rutledge. I wonder about him."

They found the former secretary of state in Fairfax, Virginia. Following the abrupt termination of his public career, George Mason University welcomed Rutledge into their faculty as a Professor of Practice in the Schar School of Policy and Government.

Chow and Holzgraf sat themselves down on a bench in the lobby of Van Metre Hall, waiting for his lecture to end.

"This will be weird," said Chow. "He got himself in trouble with all those remarks about the bots saving us from ourselves. *What if*— you know?"

"I do. My worry? When he evaporates, we are going to look like murderers."

Classroom doors opened wide, and a crowd of chattering students made their exit. Chow and Holzgraf stood up, waiting for the distinguished diplomat to show. When he did, five minutes later, his face brightened with happy recognition.

"Nice to see you two. Holly Chow, right? And Guy Holzgraf, I believe. How are the nation's heroic gunsmiths these days?"

Chow pointed her waver at him. He backed away with his hands raised to ward off the rays. His face was white.

She pulled the trigger.

Whoooosh

But the former diplomat did not dissolve.

"What the hell?" He clapped a hand over his chest. He was gasping for breath. "My ticker isn't what it was."

Holzgraf helped the old man to a chair. "Sorry, sir. We're just testing, making sure we've got all the bots."

"Jesus. My passport is up-to-date, thank you very much."

Next stop, New York. A call to General Upshaw revealed that Ambassador Gavrilov, the final living member of the notorious tour, was speaking at the United Nations.

"So it's gotta be the Russian dude."

"Pretty sneaky, right?"

"We should have guessed right away."

They hailed a cab. Holzgraf dug around in his wallet and came up with an ITF business card. He scrawled a note on it.

"What's that?"

"Mo put in a word for us, set up the meeting, but this is our calling card."

"Oh. It says we have a gift for tour members."

"We do. Ever see *North by Northwest?*"

"Hitchcock movie, I heard of it."

"Right — I'm going to play the Cary Grant role."

Ambassador Gavrilov came out of his office in the Secretariat building's Russian suite to greet the pair. The place was lightly populated by visitors, actual secretaries, and guards.

"Zdravstvuyte, deti. How may I help the young heroes? A glass of *tchai,* perhaps? Come in, we talk."

Holzgraf produced the wave gun and aimed it.

The weapon looked like a Tokarev pistol to Gavrilov. He staggered backward.

"Bozhe moy! Help! Assassins!"

Two buff guards were quick to grab Holzgraf. They wrestled him to the ground. On the way down he pulled the trigger.

Buuuzzz

The wave gun sprayed the Russian ambassador with just the right combination of microwaves to dissolve any bot or sando. But once again, results were negative. Like the other starbase tourists, he was just an individual human being after all. In his case with a sovereign country to represent, a wife back home in a Moscow apartment, a daughter, a son, a long list of friends, a half-finished piano sonata, and his own views on life.

Several phone calls were required, but all charges against Chow and Holzgraf were eventually dropped. While they were cooling their heels in New York's 17th precinct jail, their thoughts turned to the future.

"Now we can finally get married," said Chow.

"Yeah," mumbled Holzgraf in a hoarse voice. His Adam's apple was still sore from the Russian guard's chokehold. "A month ago it looked like our Big Adventure. Now it seems . . ."

". . . anticlimactic, I know. What about our honeymoon? Where shall we go?"

Holzgraf turned and kissed his fiancée.

"Not here."

Tom Wagstaff, his wife Marianne Sarzeau, and their precocious son Gabriel returned to Applefield, California, in a state of exhaustion after long flights and longer layovers. It was dark when they arrived in nearby Tarvolo, where Tom's mother Lorraine handed over their sleeping daughter Rachel.

Promises were made to catch up very soon, and the family motored home.

As soon as their luggage was safely stashed in their loft's only closet, Wagstaff raced to his desk and began typing furiously on his computer.

"Hey, hon, bedtime," said Marianne through a yawn.

She leaned over her husband's shoulder to peek at his work. "What are you doing, anyway?"

"Got to get the paper out. It's way overdue."

"Can't it wait until tomorrow?"

"Are you kidding? I've got a story to tell!"

50

AFTER MUCH DEBATE involving various levels of government and various possessive stakeholders, a decision was made to move the alien cube — presumably an engine — into NORAD's bomb-proof bunker under Cheyenne Mountain in Colorado.

A research program was organized to understand the cube's purpose and inner workings. Because the IRIS Corporation was a safe government think tank, and because he was the company's chief technical analyst, Roman Garibaldi, Ph.D., was put in charge. His friends and colleagues at the alphabet agencies, NITCOM, FULTAP, and ITF, were well pleased.

For the first few months he and his associate Jorge Asturias, a roly-poly physicist representing Mexico's interests, spent all their time analyzing the little circular pads placed flush with the titanium surface of the cube. In all, they documented twelve of them.

Garibaldi was perplexed. "Why a dozen? Why not eight? Or sixteen?"

"Counting systems often go by digits. How many fingers did those *viejos* have on each arm, actually?" queried Asturias.

"All we saw were desiccated corpses. In the pictures, they had two."

"Mmm. Quaternary notation?"

Voltmeters revealed electrical signals pulsing mysteriously through those pads at right around five volts. Two of the pads were more potent, however — they fried the voltmeter at a thousand volts. The pulse rates varied inscrutably from pad to pad. Garibaldi and Asturias wrote it all down.

They requisitioned an ultrasound machine and got themselves a good, albeit low resolution, view of the cube's interior, pinpointing the size and location of the various enigmatic parts, and the puzzling torus that seemed to be spinning.

"This thing is two hundred thousand years old," mumbled Garibaldi. "Yet old Brom drew all his laser power from it. Nobody's batteries last that long."

Asturias scratched his head. "It is obvious — the cube must draw its energy from the vacuum foam."

"But how? We figure that out . . ."

". . . and we become *héroes de bigtime, si?*"

Following a period of detailed study, they decided to run a test loop from one of the electrical pads to another one on the opposite side of the cube. They picked the pair because their pulse rates matched.

As it happened, a very curious Nancy Weatherall arrived in their secure laboratory to watch.

Garibaldi made the connections — magnetically, no solder required — and Asturias applied a voltage.

Weatherall let out a shriek and dodged aside as the cube magically abandoned its position in the center of the laboratory and buried itself in a rocky wall fifteen feet away, smashing through a shelf of test equipment in the process. Shards of plywood and plaster and stone flew all over the place.

"Note to self: five volts across pads three and eleven cause horizontal translation," muttered Garibaldi.

Then the result hit home, and all three jittery scientists burst out laughing.

"See what we did! My God, it moves!"

Weatherall brushed away plaster dust. "Yes it does. I'm going home before it explodes."

▼

Cautious experiments followed; experiments involving various minute voltages, applied at very short intervals, to carefully chosen pads. After more months of work, Garibaldi and Asturias were reasonably sure that they knew what they were doing. They planned another series of tests for the following year.

Their plans were short-circuited, as it were, by a visit from Barney Wyatt, who griped over the lack of progress and demanded to see some action on behalf of the President's National Security Council.

"We show him a vertical elevation," suggested Asturias. "Pads five and nine."

"Okay. One millisecond pulse at three volts, *comprende?*"

"*Si, Señor!*"

Wyatt examined the cube. "These little black pads, they're electrical?'

"Yup, just like the connectors on your laptop."

"I'll be damned." Wyatt traced a finger over the titanium surface. "Not very big, is it? A yard across at most. So, is this an engine of some kind? Do we know at least that much?"

Garibaldi shrugged. "Definitely not a refrigerator. We're still experimenting."

"Well, show me something I can retail to the President."

Asturias handed a pair of goggles, a mountain climber's helmet, and a kevlar flak jacket to their visitor. He and Garibaldi donned the same gear.

"Just in case," said Garibaldi with a reassuring smile.

"Is this really necessary?"

"First time we tried a control input, it was like a car accident — *kaboom.*"

"Oh." Wyatt put on the protective equipment.

"Now stand back, behind that shield."

Wyatt retreated behind a heavy plexiglass room divider. Garibaldi and Asturias joined him there.

"Ready? We're going to raise the cube just about one foot. Five, four, three, two, one . . ."

Asturias pressed a button.

The cube vanished.

An immense cascade of bedrock fell down through a yard-wide hole blown through the ceiling.

"Good God!" said Wyatt.

Once he was sure all the rock fragments that were going to fall had already fallen, Garibaldi cautiously worked his way over the pile of rubble to a spot underneath the hole. He stared upward all the way to daylight, several hundred feet above.

"Helluva tunnel over here. With a light at the end — *sky!*"

An Air Force helicopter lifted the three men up the eastward facing slope of Cheyenne Mountain. Garibaldi trained binoculars on the forested terrain and searched anxiously for signs of the cube. They flew back and forth over the most likely areas. On the third pass Wyatt spotted broken tree limbs and a faint plume of dust, like smoke from a chimney.

"Down there! See?"

The helicopter crew winched the researchers and their visitor down to an open patch on the mountain in a rescue basket.

The trio made their way through tall pines and firs to the cube's exit location by a circuitous route. They could hardly see beyond the nearest trees and had to rely on the helicopter for directions.

Finally, covered with scratches and pine pitch, they arrived at a rough hole in the ground. Hovering above it was the cube, floating in place just out of reach.

"Jesus, the thing is levitating."

Garibaldi peered down into the hole. He could see the bright lights of his lab shining far below.

"Okay, let's get a net over this hole, and tie something onto the cube, so it can't fall."

One of the aircrew, an athletic young woman looking like an astronaut in helmet, goggles, and jumpsuit, descended on the winch cable. She tossed a cargo net to the men below and moved the rescue basket underneath the cube itself.

"What is this thing, anyway?" she asked.

"Interstellar faster-than-light drive. We're testing it."

The woman laughed. "What is it — really?"

"Oh, prototype guidance system. Shock test got out of hand."

The woman made a thumbs-up sign. "Sure hope the Russians don't have one of these."

"Pretty sure we've got the jump on the Russians this time."

Asturias covered the hole with the cargo net and fastened it to the ground with steel pins and a hammer.

Garibaldi spun a finger in the air to direct the helicopter crew. "Haul away," he called out.

The pilot ramped up the collective pitch of the rotors, and the helicopter started to rise. The cable between the chopper and the cube became taught. But straining with all its horsepower, the helicopter could not budge the cube.

"Well, shit. It's stuck."

"Stuck in mid air. How the hell?"

Suddenly, whatever force was holding the cube in place let go, and the helicopter jumped two hundred feet into the sky. The rescue basket with the cube and woman aboard gyrated dizzily, spinning around and around, oscillating back and forth.

"Oh my God!" cried Garibaldi, holding his head in his hands.

The pilot slowly regained control and gently lowered the bouncing cube to within reach of the men on the ground. Looking pale, the crew woman eased herself off the rescue basket.

Garibaldi clambered up to take her place.

"Gotta keep an eye on this thing. You guys get the next lift."

▼

Soon the cube was safely back on its bench in the NORAD bunker, apparently none the worse for wear.

Wyatt stared balefully at the thing. Garibaldi took note of his obvious skepticism.

"Don't worry, we're making progress. Isn't that right, Jorge?"

Asturias made a face. *"Cierto, Doctor . . ."*

"Barney, you saw the translation — spectacular, right?"

Wyatt pointed at the hole in the ceiling. "This is what we get for a year of research? A hole? An unsolvable puzzle?"

Garibaldi hiked himself up on the table holding the cube. He rested his arm on its surface in a casual embrace.

"It's not unsolvable."

Wyatt irritably paced the room. "All right. The question in my mind is, do we have the right team on this? The Prez wants results, wants to announce we've decoded the cube as a way to frame this whole ugly experience, reassure America — make that the world — and its citizens. Declare victory with some optimism."

Garibaldi picked up a screwdriver and tossed it back and forth from hand to hand.

"Listen, Barney, we like to think we move fast in the modern world, but not everything happens overnight. The Greeks invented windmills before the time of Christ our savior. They didn't take hold until the middle ages. The Chinese invented rockets a thousand years ago. It took another thousand years for their big idea to put us on the Moon."

"What's that mean?"

"The cube, possibly an engine, is based on a civilization and technology that is far, far beyond us. We will figure it out, of that I am certain — but it might take a while."

"Okay, how long you think?"

"I dunno. A thousand years?"